The Secret Life of Maeve Lee Kwong is a companion to *Bridie's Fire*, *Becoming Billy Dare* and *A Prayer for Blue Delaney*. Each tells a vivid, self-contained story, and can be read on its own. Together, the four books make up the captivating CHILDREN OF THE WIND series, exploring 150 years of Australian life through the adventures of four feisty young people.

'I loved being in the secret world of Maeve, a place rich in laughter and tears, ghosts and surprises – all the right ingredients for a terrific read.'
Brigid Lowry

'Kirsty Murray understands families, joy and the relentlessness of grief. This is a stirring story, rigorously researched so that each detail feels true.'
Alyssa Brugman

PRAISE FOR KIRSTY MURRAY'S EARLIER BOOKS

'Rich with Australian history.'
Australian Bookseller and Publisher

'I've just finished *Bridie's Fire*. I loved it!'
Georgia, aged 13

'Full of incident, adventure and rich detail.'
Viewpoint

'I really love this series; the books have so much insight. I recommend *A Prayer for Blue Delaney* for people in the early years of high school right up to the age when you start losing your sight – very hard to put down.'
Carmel, Year 11

KIRSTY MURRAY is a fifth-generation Australian whose ancestors came from Ireland, Scotland, England and Germany. Some of their stories provided her with the backcloth for the CHILDREN OF THE WIND series. Kirsty lives in Melbourne with her husband and a gang of teenagers.

KIRSTY MURRAY

Children of the Wind

The Secret Life of Maeve Lee Kwong

ALLEN&UNWIN

First published in 2006

Copyright © Kirsty Murray 2006

Allen & Unwin
83 Alexander Street
Crows Nest NSW 2065
Australia
Phone: (61 2) 8425 0100
Fax: (61 2) 9906 2218
Email: info@allenandunwin.com
Web: www.allenandunwin.com

National Library of Australia
Cataloguing-in-Publication entry:
Murray, Kirsty.
The secret life of Maeve Lee Kwong.

ISBN 978 1 86508 737 5
ISBN 1 86508 737 8.

I. Title. (Series: Murray, Kirsty. Children of the wind).

A823.3

This project has been assisted by the Commonwealth Government through the Australia Council, its arts funding and advisory body

Series designed by Ruth Grüner
Cover image by Pigs Might Fly
Set in 10.7 pt Sabon by Ruth Grüner
Printed by McPherson's Printing Group, Maryborough, Victoria

1 3 5 7 9 10 8 6 4 2

Teachers' notes available from www.allenandunwin.com

Contents

Acknowledgements

It's easy to imagine that writing a contemporary novel would require less research than a work of historical fiction. When I began writing Maeve's story, I assumed I knew my own time so well that I wouldn't need to conduct much research. But I was wrong. Many people both knowingly and unknowingly assisted me in putting Maeve's story together. I would particularly like to thank the following:

For their guidance and inspiration, Gabrielle Wang and Mabel Wang; for their insights into the lives of modern girls, Lauren Magner, Alice Boyle, Roxane Walker, Niki Minster, and Jocelyn Ainslie; Sandy Yao for the inspiration provided by her story 'The Mysterious Calendar'; Danny Saks and Janie Forbes, Tim Clarke and Heidi O'Neill, Alice Perceval, David Allen, Jill Delbridge and Ferg Fricke, and Margaret Hoctor for their hospitality and support; Janie Barker for advice on clairvoyance; Patrick Sutton of the Gaiety School of Theatre, Dublin, for explaining his vigorous approach to drama and Irish theatre; staff and students of Saint Scholastica's College, Sydney, especially Bec, Lorraine, Mary-anne, Emma, Stephanie, Katie, Samantha, Mel and Kayla; Dana Duncan and the Drama department of Methodist Ladies College, Melbourne; also special thanks to Ros Price and Sarah Brenan of Allen & Unwin for their support and their always refreshing good faith. I would also like to acknowledge the Australia Council for its financial support.

The snatches of poetry that Sue recites to Maeve are from 'The Old Age of Queen Maeve' by William Butler Yeats and 'For Maeve' by Mervyn Peake. The play that the girls rehearse with Patrick Cassidy is 'Waiting for Godot' by Samuel Beckett.

Sometimes, particularly when writing, it's easy to forget that we are all bound by the laws of physics, caught in a moment in time. Thanks to my fellow time travellers who have endured, informed and influenced this book at every step, my ever obliging family: Elwyn, Billy and Ruby Murray, Ken, Bella, Romanie and Theo Harper.

For Kenneth Harper,
my secret-keeper,
with love

I

Hungry ghosts

'So – time to talk to the dead!' said Maeve. She flipped open the ouija board and set it in front of her friends. In the glow of the bedside lamp, Stephanie's eyes shone with excitement, but Bianca sat on a pile of doonas chewing the ends of her long blonde hair and frowning.

'I'm not sure I want to do this,' she said. 'Remember *The Exorcist*?'

Maeve laughed. 'Hey Bunka, it's okay. You could look cool with your head on backwards!'

'We're not *speaking* to the dead,' said Steph, pushing pillows and cushions away from the ouija board. 'They're just going to send us some messages. You know, they're on "the other side", sort of outside time, so they can see the future.'

Maeve smiled and winked at Bianca. Steph always took anything to do with fortune-telling way too seriously.

'It's so bright in here,' said Stephanie. 'No spirits are going to show with the place lit up like this. We need total darkness.'

'How are we meant to read the ouija board if there's no light?' asked Bianca.

'Candlelight, remember!' said Stephanie. 'Don't tell me you forgot to bring the extras, Bunka!'

Bianca rustled around in her backpack and pulled out two fat pink candles while Maeve gathered all the tea-lights scattered along her shelves and set them in a circle on the floor. It felt more like a fairy party than a séance.

Bianca wrapped her doona around her head like a hood. 'Omigod! This is so like something out of *Charmed* or that Wicca film. I am so spooked.'

'Yeah, we might scare up some hungry ghosts,' said Maeve.

'Hungry ghosts?'

'They're Chinese ghosts, spirits with tiny little mouths and great big stomachs full of fire, and my grandmother reckons they are deeply pissed off with the living.'

Bianca let out a squeal and pulled the doona over her head completely.

'Bunka,' pleaded Steph. 'Cut the scaredy-cat crap. I know you're faking.'

'I think I'll turn out the hall lights,' said Maeve. She tiptoed past her little brother's bedroom, switched off the light that hung over the stairway and then hurried back to her room. 'Hope Mum doesn't spring us,' she said. 'She'll definitely wreck the mood. She is a total sceptic.'

Bianca giggled. 'My mum would probably want to join us. She's such an old hippy.'

'Definitely no mothers allowed,' said Steph. They wriggled in closer together until all their knees were touching.

Maeve glanced through the list of instructions. 'Where's the planchette?'

'The what?' asked Steph.

'It says here in the instructions that there's meant to be a "planchette" that we all put our fingers on.'

'Tim lost it on school camp. He said we can use a glass upside down. That's just as good. But first we have to do something to invoke the spirits.'

'Like what?' asked Bianca.

'We have to chant "power words" to attract something into the room.'

'Like "Josh Whitton is gorgeous, Josh Whitton's a spunk",' said Maeve.

Bianca covered her mouth to hide her smile. 'I could so handle attracting him into the room.'

'Get serious, you two,' said Steph.

'How about *Om mani padme hum*,' said Bianca, humming the last word.

'That sounds like some sort of hippy chant.'

'So, it's still kinda magic. My mum says it when she's meditating. At least it should attract a good spirit.'

Stephanie shrugged. 'It can't hurt to try,' she said. Together they all chanted the mantra. '*Om mani padme hummmmmm.*'

'Now, we all have to put our fingertips on the edge of the glass, like this.'

Stephanie centred the glass on the battered ouija board. Maeve wondered how it was going to slide across the scratched surface. There were two arcs of letters, a row of numbers and 'GOODBYE' written across the bottom of the board. In the top right-hand corner there was a picture of a crescent moon and 'NO' in big letters. In the opposite corner there was a smiling sun and the word 'YES'.

For a long moment, they were all silent, waiting for something to happen.

'Is there anyone out there?' Stephanie tried to make her voice sound deep and magical, but she choked on the last word and it came out squeaky.

Maeve bit her lip to stifle the laughter that kept threatening to burst out. But suddenly the glass began to move.

'Are you pushing it, Steph?' she asked.

'No, shhhhh . . .'

The three girls leant in closer as the glass slid across the ouija board to the smiling sun and the word 'YES'.

Bianca caught her breath. 'Are you a friendly spirit?' she asked.

The glass began to move towards 'NO' on the opposite side of the board. Maeve wanted to snatch her hand away but it felt as if her fingertips were fused to the glass. She looked across at Stephanie, trying to decide whether her friend was guiding it or whether it really was moving of its own volition. Suddenly, the glass veered around again and headed back towards 'YES'. They all sighed with relief.

'Think of good questions,' whispered Steph.

'Who does Josh Whitton really like?' asked Bianca.

The glass moved down to the letters on the ouija board and stopped over the letter 'B' then headed determinedly towards 'I'.

'You're pushing the glass, Bianca,' said Stephanie.

'I am not!'

It took a few minutes for the board to spell out Bianca's name.

Steph rolled her eyes and then leant forward, as if she

were speaking to the board. 'Will I be famous and find success as an actress?'

The glass moved quickly towards 'YES'. Steph smiled. 'You ask next,' she said, nodding at Maeve.

Maeve tried to think what to ask. She didn't really want a boyfriend yet and she didn't know if she liked the idea of being famous. She bit her lower lip, trying to come up with a good question.

'Will all my dreams come true?' she asked finally.

The glass began to glide across the board, circling the letters in the middle and then it looked as if it was going to dip down towards 'GOODBYE'. Maeve felt annoyed that she'd asked such a lame question. Now she wasn't even going to get an answer. Suddenly, the glass started to twitch. It was as if two opposing forces were trying to move it in different directions. Maeve tried to let go, but before she could, there was a popping noise and the glass exploded beneath their fingertips.

Bianca screamed, the room was plunged into darkness and Maeve felt a slicing pain in her finger.

Steph leapt up and switched on the overhead light. Maeve held her hand up to show a drop of red blood beading on her fingertip. 'Check this out. I thought it said it was a good spirit!' she said shakily.

'Tim told me sometimes things can go weird,' said Steph. 'He said his friend Damien got a bad spirit who told the séance about all the evil stuff that Damien had been doing behind everyone's backs, but . . . nothing like this.'

From the next room, Ned set up a wail. There were footsteps in the hall. Maeve quickly dropped her pillow over the board and the fragments of broken glass.

'Is everything all right in here?' asked her mother, opening the door and peering into the bedroom. She held Ned on one hip, cradling his head against her shoulder.

'Fine, Mum. We were just mucking around.'

'You need to keep the volume down. You woke Ned. And it's getting late, girls. You've all got dance in the morning so it's time you switched off. I don't want to have to come and tell you again.'

When the door closed, Maeve hurriedly picked up the board and tipped the broken glass into her wastepaper basket. No one spoke as they settled down into their makeshift beds on the floor.

'That was too weird,' said Bianca, her voice small in the darkness.

'I feel a little bit freaked,' said Steph.

'Let's try not to think about it,' said Maeve. 'We'll all feel better in the morning.' She put an arm around each of her friends and drew them closer.

There was a long silence and then Bianca whispered, 'It's okay for now, but what about tomorrow night when I'm in my own bed and you guys aren't around to make me feel safe? Then I'll really flip out.'

'Hey,' said Maeve, turning on the bedside lamp. 'I've got an idea.'

She pulled open her desk drawer, took out a pair of scissors and handed them to Bianca. 'Friendship braids,' she said. 'That's what we need. What we do is braid a really skinny plait into everyone's hair. That way, when you're by yourself tomorrow night you can wrap it round your finger and know that we're out there. Sort of like a lucky charm.'

Maeve brushed her dark hair forward. 'Cut,' she said.

Bianca snipped with the scissors. The cold metal made Maeve's skin prickle.

'Got it.' Bianca held up a strand of Maeve's silky hair.

'Cool. Now you let me cut some of yours, and then we'll do Steph.'

Bianca knelt in front of them both, her long blonde hair spread in a fan across the pillow. Maeve cut a lock from the nape of her neck and held it up to check it was the same length as her own. Then she cut a ringlet from Steph's thick red-gold curls.

She set the three locks of hair in a row on her dresser and divided them into piles. Maeve's long hair was brownish-black in winter, but in summer the sun touched it with dark gold streaks so that it glowed like rich, dark chocolate. Steph's hair was a curly, gingery mane with bright red highlights and Bianca's hair was white-gold. When they walked with their arms linked and their heads together, they made a perfect combination. Ever since primary school, everyone had joked that Maeve, Bianca and Steph were like a bowl of Neapolitan ice-cream; Balmain's triple treat of chocolate, strawberry and vanilla.

They sat in a tight triangle, each braiding the two opposing colours into the other's hair where the single tress had been cut. 'Now, no matter what happens, we're tangled up with each other,' said Maeve. 'Three in one and one in three. If you get scared, you know that you can always count on your best friends. Always.'

2

God's athletes

Sunlight streamed in through the bedroom window as Maeve angled the tweezers and carefully lifted out the shard of glass that was still lodged in her fingertip. Bianca turned away from the mirror.

'That was really freaky, what happened last night.'

'We were probably all pushing too hard and the glass was bodgy,' said Maeve.

'No, I think it was trying to tell us something,' said Steph.

Maeve shrugged. 'Like what?'

'I don't know. Maybe something really big and important is going to happen. Maybe something like 9/11 right here in Sydney. I hate not knowing the future.'

Maeve looked out the window at a tiny triangle of Sydney Harbour, the blue water shimmering in the sunlight. It felt as if last night had happened to someone else.

'I know exactly what's next,' she said. 'My mum is going to be seriously pissed off 'cause we'll be late getting out the door and Louise will yell at us for missing the warm-ups. Look, it's a perfect day, so chill, Steph.'

In the kitchen, Ned sat in his highchair carefully

squishing cubes of cut fruit between his fingers and then sucking the squashy mess from his hands. He crowed with happiness as soon as he set eyes on Maeve. The next instant, he swept the remains of his breakfast onto the floor and stood up as if he was about to dive into her arms. She lifted him out of the highchair and snuggled him on her lap.

Sue set a plate stacked with buttermilk pancakes in the middle of the table.

'You'll get covered in mashed banana if you're not careful. Try not to get it on your leotard.'

'Hey boofba,' said Steph, tweaking Ned's nose. He looked up at her and grinned.

'He's not a boofhead,' said Maeve, stroking his silky dark hair and kissing the top of his head. 'Ned's a gorgeous little monkey. Born in the Chinese Year of the Monkey, weren't you, cheeky boy.'

'It's okay, Maeve. In our family, boofba means "bewdiful boy". It's a compliment.'

'He doesn't need any more compliments,' said Bianca, tipping maple syrup over her pancakes. 'Look at what a fat pudding head he has already. As if there aren't enough conceited boys in the world.'

Maeve nuzzled Ned's sticky cheek. 'Don't listen to her,' she whispered in his ear. 'You are perfect.'

'Give me that boy,' said Sue. 'You lot will never get out the door at this rate. I need you all to try the new costumes on before you leave.'

She whisked Ned away from Maeve and took him out to Andy, sitting in the sunshine on the back verandah with the Saturday papers spread around him. Maeve watched as

Ned bounced up and down in Andy's arms. It was weird how much he looked like Andy. Yet everyone said she and Ned looked alike, even if they did have different fathers. They both had the same confusing mix of Asian and European features; skin like pale honey, a spray of freckles across their noses and the same brown eyes flecked with gold and green.

Sue came back in, gathering her thick black hair into a ponytail. It made her look like a teenager, as if she wasn't much older than Maeve.

'Okay, team,' she said. 'Down to the studio for a fitting.'

Maeve quickly finished her orange juice and the three girls followed Sue to her studio under the house. Three shimmering white costumes lay beside the sewing machine. Sue had spent hours every evening stitching pearly sequins onto the lycra and making floaty, gossamer sleeves from white chiffon. The girls slipped into the outfits and stood in front of Sue while she adjusted the seams of each leotard. Then she stood back, tipped her head to one side and smiled.

'I know exactly what Einstein meant when he said "Dancers are the athletes of God". You three look like angels. I can't wait to see you dancing in the Christmas concert.'

Sue never missed any of Maeve's performances. She always booked front-row seats, and at the end of the show she was always waiting at the stage door with a bunch of flowers, her face alight with pride.

'Thanks a million, Sue. My mum would go mental if she had to make this,' said Steph.

Bianca stretched her hands over her head and twirled in a circle so the sequins caught the sun and sent tiny rainbow prisms of light whirling around the studio. 'Thank you, thank you, thank you,' she sang as she came to a stop. 'We all look so gorgeous! Especially me!'

Sue laughed and tousled Bianca's hair. 'Is there no end to your vanity, Bianca?'

'Not that I can see,' Bianca replied.

Maeve smiled. 'Thanks, Mum. These are the best costumes ever.'

She put her arms around her mother and kissed her on the cheek. Bianca and Steph jumped forward and hugged her as well. 'Just like having triplets!' said Sue, laughing.

'Your Mum is so cool,' said Bianca, as they pulled the front door shut behind them. 'I wish we really were triplets and all lived here.'

'Our mums are great too, even if they can't sew,' said Steph.

'Sure, but Maeve's mum is funky. I love her studio – all those piles of fabric, and rows of brushes and paint and all those colours and spangly stuff. She's a legend.'

Maeve laughed and swung her dance bag in an arc over her head. They ran up Darling Street towards the old school hall where their Saturday classes were held.

Sun streamed in through the arched casement windows and made the dark wood floor gleam in the morning light. A warm breeze drifted in through the open doors and the fans above spun lazily as Maeve picked her way through the clutter of dance bags strewn across the stage, searching for a space of her own. She unlaced her runners and buckled on her tap shoes.

Students poured in through the side door, throwing their gear onto the stage. Louise, the head of the dance school, herded a crowd of little girls in pale pink tights towards the stairs while the senior tap class began their warm-up. There were a dozen girls and five boys in the class. The sound of their tap shoes ricocheted around the hall as they stepped into line. Maeve, Steph and Bianca stood at the back. They'd only been dancing with the senior class since the beginning of second term and they watched the moves of the older students carefully.

In the break between tap and jazz, everyone dived into their bags to retrieve chips or lollies and their drink bottles. Maeve rubbed her palms along her black shorts, feeling heat radiate through the thin lycra.

'Who do you reckon he is?' asked Bianca, gesturing into the hall.

A tall, dark-haired boy in a white singlet and long black board shorts stood by the piano talking to Josh.

'I don't know. He must be new,' said Maeve.

'Fresh,' said Bianca.

'What about Josh?' asked Steph.

'What about him?' said Bianca, grinning. 'I can check out whoever I want. I mean, it's not like Josh is my boyfriend. Yet. And even if he was, I'm allowed to look, aren't I?'

'I hate it when you talk like that,' said Steph. 'You sound like a total bimbo.'

'You're just jealous,' said Bianca, tipping her head back to take a swig of water.

Maeve could sense the tension rising between her friends, like the bad feeling she'd had before the glass exploded the night before. She was glad when Louise shouted at them all to take their positions for the jazz lesson. She leapt off the stage and cartwheeled across the hall.

The warm-up for jazz was always long and gruelling. The boys groaned loudly as Louise tried to get everyone to do the splits. Maeve slid down to the floor easily. She twisted and turned, feeling the tension and release as she stretched her muscles as far as they could go. She could feel the music throbbing up through the floor and she shut her eyes, savouring the sensation.

Louise put an instrumental version of Rob Thomas's 'This is How a Heart Breaks' on the CD player and they did their first run through the routine.

'C'mon, kids. You can work harder than this. You know we've only got six weeks until the Christmas show, and we have to get these routines tight.'

Maeve bit her lip and concentrated, then let the music take hold. On either side of her, Steph and Bianca fell into the rhythm. As if in prayer, the three of them were bound to the dance. Maeve loved that moment in time when their bodies moved in perfect harmony. They were in sync again – the arguments, the tension, the exploding glass, every bad thing swept away by the music.

3

Keep it sweet

Outside, after the class, the girls flopped down in the cool green grass beneath the date palms.

Josh and the new boy came out and walked past the girls as if they weren't even there, but Maeve saw Josh glance back over his shoulder and smile at Bianca.

'Say something interesting, something intelligent that's going to make him think I'm really too busy to notice him,' whispered Bianca.

'Why?' said Maeve. 'You are totally aware of everything he does.'

'Not the point, dummy. I want him to try harder.'

'I don't think Josh has ever tried hard to do anything,' said Steph. 'I wouldn't hold my breath waiting for him to please you.'

'Not Josh, the other guy, the cute one.'

'You mean Omar,' said Steph.

'How do you know his name?' asked Bianca.

'He plays footy with Josh and Tim. I think Josh talked him into coming. They do break-dancing together too. Or something like that. Footy-playing break-dancers.' Steph laughed.

'Why didn't you tell me before?'

'I didn't want to encourage you.'

Bianca stuck her tongue out at Steph.

'Hey, Omar!' yelled Bianca. 'See you next week.'

Omar turned and gave her a brilliant smile.

'Did you see that?' asked Bianca.

Maeve laughed. 'You are so classic.'

She pulled out her mobile and called home to tell her mum that they were finished and about to head off to Newtown. It was only in the past few weeks that Sue had agreed to let Maeve go outside Balmain without her.

The three girls swung onto the bus and squashed up in a seat made for two. Bianca plunged around in the bottom of her backpack and pulled out a silk leopard-print bag. 'Check this out. Only thirty dollars.'

'I've seen them for twenty bucks at Balmain Market,' said Steph.

Bianca looked blank and stuffed the bag away. 'Well, I thought it was cool.'

'It is cool. It's just you paid too much for it,' said Steph. 'But then, you can afford it, I guess.'

Maeve put a hand on Steph's arm to stop her saying anything else. Bianca didn't think she was rich but her house in Birchgrove had sweeping views over the harbour and her parents gave her more pocket money than any girl in Year 8.

'Did you get one of these?' asked Bianca, pulling out a small card with a picture of two girls dressed in pink, their arms wrapped around each other.

'No way! Jess Turner's sixteenth birthday party! She said that she was being so "exclusive" she wasn't inviting anyone in Year 8.'

'Well, she invited me,' said Bianca.

'Who's Alanna?' asked Maeve.

'She's at Balmain High,' said Steph. 'She's Jess's step-sister – and her best friend, or so she says. They are truly annoying, the pair of them.'

Maeve could feel trouble brewing again. Trying not to meet Steph's disapproving gaze, she took the invitation from Bianca and turned it over. The card was pale pink with gold stars announcing the details of the party on the back.

'"No pressies, no entry",' read Maeve. ' "Party in pink. Finger food. BYO limited alcohol." What do they mean, limited?'

'They are totally under-age,' said Steph. 'How can they even have that on their invites? I mean, sneaking booze in is one thing but advertising sneaking it in! Tacky.'

'Do you have to be so anal?' snapped Bianca. 'If you were the one invited, you wouldn't be so picky.'

'I'm not being picky. Even if I wanted to go, I wouldn't be allowed if my parents saw this invite,' said Steph.

'I wouldn't be able to go even if Mum didn't see it,' said Maeve.

'Neither of you were invited, so it doesn't matter, does it?'

Maeve and Steph exchanged glances. Maeve linked arms with both her friends and dragged them to their feet. 'Then me and Steph need some serious retail therapy as consolation. C'mon – let's shop.'

Maeve had been to Newtown with her mum more times than she could count, but somehow it felt different being there with Steph and Bianca. With Sue, she had to spend ages hanging around in the button shop while her mother sorted out what she needed for her next design or picked through piles of fabric looking for the best offcuts of coloured silks. Today she wouldn't have to go anywhere she didn't want to. It was as if she was in charge of her own life – and it felt good.

They wandered down King Street, window-shopping and traipsing in and out of funky clothes boutiques. As they walked west along the street, they passed Newtown Secondary School of Performing Arts.

'I so want to go there for HSC,' said Bianca wistfully. 'But Dad won't let me. He said I had to keep my options open. I know already I only want to sing. I can't believe he wouldn't let me even audition. And Mum was pathetic and said she thought he had a point. When I think I could have gone there instead of St Philomena's! No uniform, no chapel, and boys as well!'

'No us, either,' said Maeve.

'Yeah, you wouldn't trade us for a bunch of grungy guys, would you?' asked Steph.

On the other side of the road, a boy on a skateboard came gliding out of the school gates and turned down King Street.

'Cute,' said Bianca, as if she hadn't even heard Steph's question. 'Bit of a short-arse, but not bad.'

'God, Bunka. You are so boy-crazy,' said Steph. 'Haven't you got anything better to think about?'

'What? Like world peace? Like you would know so much about it with a brother fighting a twisted war in Iraq!' Bianca tossed her hair over her shoulder.

Steph blushed angrily. Quickly Maeve stepped between

them. 'Let's cool it. We're meant to be having fun. Why don't we go and get a granita?'

She slipped her arms around their shoulders and tugged at the friendship braids. 'Keep it sweet, guys. Triple treat, remember?'

4

Sudden and laughing

Maeve and Steph ran all the way up the hill and arrived at school breathless. It always happened when Maeve dropped by Steph's house on the way to the bus stop. Maeve loved the cheerful chaos of the Maguire household, the football boots scattered along the hall, the noisy arguments between Steph and her brothers, but somehow they always managed to miss the bus.

St Philomena's stood on the top of a hill in a street lined with narrow terrace houses. Lush green lawns rolled down in front of the old Victorian mansion that now was home to a few elderly nuns. Purple and white jacaranda blossom lay scattered across the grass and the flowerbeds that curved around the pathways were ablaze with roses. Maeve pushed open the heavy cast-iron gate and they ran along the path, sending a flutter of rose petals into the warm morning air.

Everyone in English was working in groups when Maeve and Steph handed their late passes to Mrs Spinelli. As soon as they joined Bianca, she leant across and whispered to Maeve in a sharp, sulky voice, 'Mum won't let me go to the party unless you come too.'

'Me? I'm not even invited!' said Maeve.

'Well, you are now. I told Jess and she said it's fine to bring you.'

'What about Steph?' whispered Maeve.

'She said her parents wouldn't let her.'

'You mean, I'm not cool enough,' said Steph bitterly.

'You know that's not why,' said Bianca.

Maeve looked from one friend to the other. 'Even if I could get permission, I don't know if I'd want to go, Bunka. I hardly know Jess.'

'Please, Maeve. I so want to go, but Mum and Dad said only if you come with me.'

'Why me?'

'Because they think you're so smart and sensible that you'll stop me doing anything stupid.'

'That shows they don't know me at all. I'm your minder, am I?'

'Please?'

'Don't get excited. I'll have to ask my mum. I'm not allowed to do parties – not at night. Not yet.'

As soon as the teacher turned away, Bianca slipped the pink invitation into Maeve's hand. 'Think about it,' she whispered into Maeve's ear. 'Please.'

Maeve clipped off the comment about alcohol at the bottom of the card and then took it downstairs and handed it to her mother. She'd already tried to get Sue to agree without seeing the invitation but Sue had been hardline. 'It can't be much of a special occasion if they haven't even handed out proper invitations. It's probably just some big, out-of-control free-for-all.'

Sue looked slightly defeated when Maeve handed her the amended card. A good sign. She turned the pink invitation over in her hand.

'Look, darling, you're only thirteen. This girl is turning sixteen. I really don't think it's appropriate.'

'I'm nearly fourteen. It's not my fault that I'm young for my year level. Besides, what's a year or two anyway?'

'No, Maeve.'

'But Mum, if you don't let me go, Bianca won't be allowed to go. So you're letting both of us down. Please. We won't stay long. We'll come home when you say.'

'Maybe you should let her go,' said Andy, looking up from the couch where he was watching *The Bill*.

'I really don't need you weighing in on this,' said Sue.

'I'm not "weighing in". But Maeve is a real teenager now. Teenagers have parties. It's a fact of life.'

Sue gave Andy the sort of look that usually finished any conversation and he turned back to the TV.

'See! You make it sound like I'm going to get into trouble or something, Mum. Like you don't trust me.'

'It's not that. I trust you. I just don't trust the world.'

'Mum! It's only a party! Do you mean you're not going to let me go to a party until I finish high school? That's insane!'

'You're not old enough to be making the sort of decisions that you need to make in those situations. Decisions that could change your life.'

'You mean you made the wrong decision at a party once? You mean having me was the wrong decision?'

Maeve knew she'd gone too far. She was definitely going to lose the argument now. She wasn't meant to know about how she was conceived.

Sue didn't miss a beat. 'I was a lot older than you, Maeve. I was an adult. There is absolutely no comparison. If you think flinging something like that at me is going to help win me over, you are even less mature than I'd given you credit for.'

Maeve groaned. She didn't care that much about the party, but she couldn't let Bianca down. 'Mum, it's probably the last party of the year. And then it will be summer and there won't be any parties. At least, not ones that I'm invited to.'

'There's always muck-up day,' said Andy, turning around again and grinning. 'We were real ratbags at my school at the end of the year. Me and the boys, we put an ad in the *Sydney Morning Herald* – "Prime real estate for sale". You know, "three hectares, ripe for redevelopment, central location". Then we put the phone number of the Principal's office. The switchboard rang hot as hell.'

'I'm only in Year 8, Andy. You don't muck up in Year 8. That's Year 12.'

'Andy, don't tell her these stories. It doesn't help,' scolded Sue.

'All work and no play makes Jack a dull boy and Maeve a crazy girl,' added Andy, not turning around to look at them this time.

'If Andy thinks it's all right, then why not? You always said that you hated the way your mum and dad stopped you from doing anything fun. And now you're even worse with me.'

'She's right, Sue. Your parents still can't leave you alone. You don't want history repeating.'

'Don't you start, Andy. At least my parents have tried to help us out.'

'Help *us* out? You mean manipulated. Manipulated you and Maeve. Bullied you into sending her to the school of their choice, not yours or hers. Nothing they do for you comes without strings attached. Everything is conditional. That's not love, that's coercion.'

Suddenly, the argument wasn't about Maeve at all. She backed away as Andy and Sue started dredging up every problem they'd ever had with her grandparents. It was always the same. Why did Andy have to bring the fight back to him every time? Now Sue would never let her go.

Maeve stormed out of the room and took the stairs two at a time. She sat on her bed with the doona over her head and tried to pretend she couldn't hear the quarrelling downstairs. She wished Andy would shut up. It wasn't as if the decision was up to him anyway. He wasn't her parent. She and Mum had been fine before he came along. Maeve remembered crying when Sue told her Andy was moving in with them. It was as if she wasn't enough for Sue.

After half an hour, the shouting from downstairs subsided and the house grew still. Maeve pulled the doona off her head and sat down at her desk, staring out the little window that looked out towards the Harbour Bridge. She pulled one of the Harry Potter books off her bookshelf and flicked through the pages, re-reading her favourite scenes at Hogwarts, half-wishing her grandparents had sent her to a boarding school.

Later that night, when Maeve had gone to bed, she heard Andy clumping down the hall to Ned's room.

That's what they did when things got really spiky after an argument. One of them would get up and sleep on the folding bed beside Ned's cot. In the morning they'd pretend that they'd slept with him because he was restless. Neither of them was a good liar.

Very faintly, Maeve could hear the sound of her mother crying. She rolled onto her side and covered her ears with her hands at first, but then she slipped out of bed and tiptoed down the hall. Sue lay curled up alone.

Maeve pulled back the doona and slipped in beside her mum. Sue was lying so still that for a moment, Maeve wondered if she was holding her breath.

'I couldn't sleep,' she whispered to her mother's back.

'I'm sorry, baby. I'm sorry if we woke you.'

'No, you didn't wake me. I couldn't sleep.'

'I hope you understand, when Andy and I have our fights. It's not about you. It's not your fault or anything.'

'It's okay. He's not my dad, anyway.'

'He does love you, Maeve.'

'Maybe. But I didn't choose him and he didn't choose me. You were the one who wanted to play happy families,' said Maeve, regretting the words as soon as they were out of her mouth.

Sue lay very still and then she turned around to face Maeve.

'You didn't choose me either.'

'Maybe I did,' replied Maeve. 'Maybe I saw you from heaven and thought, there's the best mum in the world. Ned thought the same thing. That's why we're here.'

Maeve could just make out a small smile on her mother's face in the dim light. 'I'm so glad you and Ned have each other. I always wanted a brother or a sister. I hope you two will always be there for each other.'

'Just wait until he's a teenager. Then we'll really start ganging up on you and Andy.'

Sue laughed. 'I hope not. And I hope you don't tell him everything either. There are some things parents like to keep to themselves. I didn't know you knew about the party when you were conceived.'

Maeve wriggled uncomfortably and slipped her hand out from under the covers. 'I'm sorry for shouting that at you. I've known for ages. I heard you telling someone once. I was sitting under the kitchen table, playing with Ned, and I heard you.'

'I guess it's good we can talk about it, Maeve,' said Sue. 'I could never talk about anything with my own mother. Or my father.'

'So tell me something different about *my* dad, my real dad.'

Sue grew quiet but Maeve knew she'd offer some small bit of information. It was a game they played, like knitting a scarf, where each time they talked a few new stitches were cast on and the scarf grew longer and more interesting. Before Andy came along, Maeve had never been able to ask her mother about her birth father, but somehow, now that he and Ned were in their lives, the past wasn't so treacherous.

'I wish I'd known him better. When I found out I was pregnant, I did try to find him, Maeve. You know that, don't you?'

'I know that, Mum.' This was always part of the process. Maeve had to reassure her mother if she was going to get her to talk about what had happened. As a young woman, Sue had fought with her parents to be allowed to go to art school and then, to their horror, she'd fallen pregnant to a stranger. It was bad enough that he wasn't from a good Chinese-Australian family but he wasn't even Australian. An Irish backpacker, a whirlwind romance, an accidental baby.

'I loved his voice. I loved the stories he told. That man, he knew so many stories. Not just about Ireland, but about all the places he'd visited. He had a way of looking at things that was different to anyone I'd ever met. He was a real traveller, not a tourist. He's probably still travelling. One day, I'll give you the letter he wrote from Nepal.'

'You never told me there was a letter.'

'It was the only one.'

Sue was silent then. Maeve knew they were wandering into dangerous territory.

'Tell me the story about how I got my name. Tell me that one again,' said Maeve, snuggling down beside her mum, pretending that she was little again.

Maeve heard Sue take a deep breath. Somehow, stories were always easier to tell in the darkness.

'Davy told me this story while we were riding a ferry across the harbour. I think that's why I remembered it so well. And it was really rough on the water that day. We were caught in a storm and Davy had his arms around me. He was reciting a poem. He had this amazing memory. He could memorise great long poems word for word.

'Something about the sound of the sea and his voice on that day stayed with me. When you were being born, I thought it was like riding a storm at sea. So as soon as you were in my arms, I looked at you and remembered the poem about the Irish queen that he'd told me on that stormy ferry ride. Maeve was a great ruler all in her own right, because in ancient times in that country, the women could be as powerful as the men. If I'd given you a Chinese name, it might have been Mu Lan.'

'Like Mulan in that Disney cartoon?'

'Not quite like the cartoon, but she was a great warrior woman, and so was Queen Maeve.'

'And you remembered the poem when you saw me?'

'I'm not like Davy, I can't memorise poetry, but I never forgot some of those lines. That Queen Maeve

> . . . had lucky eyes and a high heart,
> And wisdom that caught fire like the dried flax,
> At need, and made her beautiful and fierce,
> Sudden and laughing.

And that was you, when you were born, you were so beautiful and fierce and then you opened your eyes and I could have sworn that you smiled at me. They say new-born babies can't see to smile, but you smiled. *Sudden and laughing.*'

'There was another poem too, wasn't there?'

'That's right. But I can only remember a snatch of the other one. There was a line that ran *'you who are the Maeve of me'*. Isn't that beautiful? And you were my Maeve, the Maeve of me. So I couldn't have called you by any other name. Even if Goong Goong and Por Por didn't like it. I was a disappointment to them, but you will never be a disappointment to me, Maeve.'

Sue took Maeve's hand and held it in a firm and loving grip.

'Then I can go to the party?' said Maeve, entwining her fingers with her mother's and holding tight.

'Maeve, don't you ever let go?'

'Nope, never. Why did you name me after a warrior queen? I had to turn out stubborn with a name like Maeve.'

Maeve heard her mother laughing in the darkness.

'Okay, chicken, you can go to the party. But I will drop you off and I will be there to pick you up at ten p.m. on the nose and not a minute later.'

'But it doesn't start until eight! That's only two hours.'

'That's two hours more than you were going to get when this conversation started. Take it or leave it.'

'Done,' said Maeve.

5

Three Musketeers

Steph was sullen as they sat at the bus stop together.

'You won't miss much,' said Maeve. 'It will be boring without you.'

'I feel like I'm missing heaps,' said Steph, flicking at the pages of her school diary. 'Bunka doesn't want me around the way she used to. It's like three's a crowd.'

'That's crazy, Steph. I know she doesn't feel that way. It's only really good when all three of us are together.'

'Don't start that triple-treat stuff again. You know things have changed. Sometimes I think I should cross over to Balmain High for Year 9. It would be a lot easier for my folks. The scholarship only covers fees and there are always extras.'

'What? Leave St Phil's! You can't!' Maeve felt her cheeks flush. Sometimes she worried it was all her fault that they were at St Philomena's and not the local high school. Maeve's grandparents had insisted that she attend St Philomena's. When Steph and Bianca discovered that Maeve had no choice they both made sure she wouldn't be alone. Steph talked her parents into letting her sit the scholarship exam so the three of them could stay together.

It would have been terrible to be split up after sharing two years of kindergarten and seven years of primary school.

'St Phil's is great, but what I really want to do in the end is be an actor. I don't need to be at St Phil's for that.'

'We have a great drama department. Ms Donahue is a legend, and you like McCabe too, don't you? I mean, he's the one who calls us the Three Musketeers. I've been thinking, maybe that's a better name for us than triple treat.'

'Are you trying to not talk about this party?'

Maeve took Steph's face in her hands and forced her to look at her squarely. 'Steph, you know what Bunka's like. This time it's me, next time it's you. We do stuff without her too. We're equal but different, that's all.'

'Okay, okay,' said Steph, her sulky expression giving way to a smile. 'I get it. Bunka's the beauty, I'm the brain, and you're the muscle in this outfit?'

Maeve hugged her and laughed. 'Just like the Three Musketeers! I looked them up on the Internet. I think you're like Aramis. He's the stylish thinker. And Bunka's like Porthos – he's the flirt.'

'So what does that leave you? You're not really muscly enough to be the strongman.'

'Well, the third one is called Athos – but he's not really like me. I mean, he has this secret past.'

'Maybe that is you!'

'Yeah, right. It's so secret not even I know about it!'

'Do I look fat in this?' asked Bianca, turning around so Maeve could check her out from behind.

'You don't look fat in anything, Bunka. You know that,' said Maeve.

'I wish we were older. I'm so over being thirteen.'

'Thirteen is okay. But fourteen will be better, I suppose.'

'No, fifteen,' said Bianca, sighing. 'Life will really start happening when we're fifteen.'

'Actually, Bunka, our life is happening right now. Like this party that we're meant to be at.'

They'd been at Jess's for nearly an hour but Bianca had spent most of that time in the bathroom, sitting on the edge of the tub looking stressed-out. Maeve told her the story of Queen Maeve and how that had helped talk her mother around, but Bianca seemed distracted by the mirror and had trouble following it.

'Bunka, can we please go back to the party now?' asked Maeve.

'I can't. I can't go out until I've decided who I like best, Josh or Omar.'

'Omar? Since when did Omar get on the radar?'

'Since Saturday. And then he said "Hi" to me when he arrived so now I am really torn.'

'No, you are really twisted. I'm going back out to the party and you can either sit here or come out with me.'

Most of the party was happening in the back yard where coloured lights were strung up along the fence. Maeve stood by the food table and picked at a plate of chips. Apart from Bianca, she didn't really know anyone. They were all in Years 9 and 10 and only half of them were from St Philomena's. She couldn't believe she'd fought so hard to get permission to come.

Maeve looked at her watch. It was only 9.30. She still

had half an hour to get through before they'd get picked up. Sue had insisted on coming in with them and talking to Jessica's mum at the beginning of the party. It had been so embarrassing. No one else had even arrived. Somehow, the tables covered in pink tablecloths and the pink fruit punch with strawberries floating in it had reassured Sue and she'd left looking cheerful. Maeve hoped she wouldn't come back inside when she came to pick them up. Things were definitely starting to look seedy. Food was spilt all over the back lawn and there was a growing pile of discarded tinnies down near the barbecue. A crowd of older kids were sitting on lounges right down the back of the yard, the tips of their cigarettes bright in the darkness. In the living room that opened onto the back porch, a dozen girls were dancing to the Black Eyed Peas with Josh Whitton in the middle. There was definitely a shortage of boys at the party.

Maeve filled a plastic cup with the punch, but after a mouthful she discreetly spat it out behind a tree.

'Are you okay?'

Maeve wiped her mouth with the back of her hand. 'Oh hi, Omar. Yeah, I'm fine. But the punch is disgusting. It was okay before, but it tastes weird now.'

'It's spiked. I saw Joe Turner pour a bottle of vodka into it.'

'My mother will flip if she finds out there's been drinking here.'

'Jessica's mum doesn't look too stoked about it either,' he said, gesturing with his head towards the back porch. A girl that Maeve didn't recognise was throwing up in a bucket while Jessica's mum, with an expression like thunder, held the girl's long hair out of the way.

'Yuk,' said Maeve.

'Yeah, gross,' added Bianca, stepping between Maeve and Omar.

'Hey, why don't you two come hang with us?' suggested Omar. 'You can get a great view across Glebe from the upstairs balcony.'

'We'd love to,' said Bianca, crooking her finger for Maeve to follow. Maeve groaned inwardly.

Upstairs, on the balcony overlooking the street, a small group sat chatting, their heads close together. Maeve hung over the railing and stared out into the night. When her mother's silvery Corolla turned into the street she felt a rush of relief.

'C'mon, Bunka. My mum is waiting for us downstairs.'

Bianca turned to Omar and touched him lightly on the arm.

'See ya round, Omar. Gotta go.'

But Omar got up and caught her as she turned to leave. Without speaking he pulled Bianca to him and kissed her. Maeve saw Bianca stiffen but she didn't pull back. Maeve didn't know where to look.

As they walked down the stairs together, Maeve whispered to Bianca, 'What was it like?'

'Kind of gross. I hate my braces. I was so worried about cutting his lips I couldn't relax. And his tongue! He tried to stick it in my mouth but it was all cold and gross and tasted like cigarettes. I think I'll have to take up smoking if I'm going to ever get used to kissing him.'

'Bianca!'

'Only kidding. Anyway, maybe I like Josh better.'

Maeve laughed. 'You are incredible. We should call you Bee instead of Bunka, buzzing from one flower to the next.'

'Queen Bee and Queen Maeve, I like it!'

6

Tunnel vision

Maeve tugged at her uniform, trying to make the zip lie straight.

'I really need a new uniform, Mum. This is so too small for me.'

Sue was trying to clean Ned's face, wiping the remnants of his breakfast away and buttoning up a new shirt. 'The school year is nearly over. You only have another six weeks. You're not going to grow much in that short a time, sweetheart. Better to wait until February, then you'll get the most wear out of the new one.'

'But it's pinching in all the wrong places,' complained Maeve. 'Ned gets a new shirt, which he doesn't even need, and I have to wait months for a new uniform.'

Suddenly, she looked up and saw how tired and unhappy her mother looked.

'Mum? Are you okay?'

'Ned's starting crèche today. I finally found him a place. Which is great. But even with an extra couple of days a week, I can't see myself earning enough to justify the cost. And then there's this Hong Kong holiday idea.'

'We can't not go on the trip, Mum. You promised. You

promised we'd go this summer holiday. Even Steph has at least been to New Zealand. I've never been anywhere, ever.'

'Maybe we should go somewhere inside Australia.'

'You just mean somewhere cheaper, don't you?'

'I don't want to have to ask your grandparents to help us out. Andy would hate it.'

'Andy! What's he got to do with it, anyway? He never wants us to go anywhere without him, that's his problem. Besides, we don't need anyone's help. Your designs are so cool. Even my friends think they're cool. You'll sell heaps before Christmas.'

'Thanks for the vote of confidence,' said Sue.

'And next year, I'll get a job. When I'm fourteen, I'll get a job in Macca's at Darling Harbour. Jessica works there. She's earned enough to go on the overseas tour next year.'

'It's okay, Maeve. You don't have to get a job the minute you're old enough. We're not that hard up.' She picked Ned up and kissed his cheek. 'I'll give you a lift, if you like.'

Maeve wasn't used to being early for school. She jumped out of the car and ran straight through the cast-iron gate, and then realised the bell wouldn't ring for another twenty minutes. By the time she turned around to wave to Ned, the Corolla was out of sight. She flung her backpack onto the grass beneath a jacaranda tree and lay down beside it. The purple blossoms looked hazy against the summery blue morning sky. Out of the corner of her eye, she saw Steph sitting near the old convent verandah, doing her homework. Maeve sat up and waved, calling her over.

'You're never here before nine. Why are you so early?' she asked, hugging Steph.

'Homework. I didn't get that book report finished. But I worked all day Sunday and I've got eighty bucks to prove it!'

'Doing what?' asked Maeve, sitting up abruptly.

'You know that florist's near the bus stop, Crazy Daisies? They've been really busy doing all these functions and they needed someone to help out. They're going to give me work every weekend, Saturday and Sunday, from now on.'

'But what about dance? You can't not come to dance! We've been going together since we were three. Remember when we were fluffy ducks at that first concert? If you miss classes, Louise might not let you dance with us.'

'I'll come to the Tuesday-night class and I'll make it some of the Saturdays,' said Steph, avoiding meeting Maeve's shocked expression. 'Anyway, you and Bianca will be fine. I mean, you two are the party animals.'

'Don't start that again. I told you that party would be crap and it was. Bianca hooked up with Omar while I stood around bored out of my brain.'

Stephanie laughed. 'That's what you get being a body-guard.'

Maeve was glad it was music class first up until she realised she'd left her flute in her mum's car. Chloe was playing clarinet at the front of the classroom, running through a long, squeaky piece of jazz. Maeve slumped lower in her seat between Steph and Bianca. 'I am so going to cop it,' she muttered. 'I don't have my flute.'

'McCabe won't give you a detention,' said Bianca.

'Yeah, but he'll make me feel really guilty. He's good at that. I'd rather get shouted at.'

'Musketeers,' said McCabe, turning around, 'I know it's Monday and you feel a compelling need to debrief on your weekends, but the rest of us are trying to listen to Chloe.'

'See what I mean?' whispered Maeve, as soon as the teacher turned away.

Steph and Bianca shook their heads, warning Maeve to be quiet, but it was too late.

'Maeve!' said McCabe, his voice sharp. 'You're next.'

'I forgot my flute,' said Maeve.

McCabe rolled his eyes and ran one hand through his thick, silvery hair. 'You can borrow one of the school's,' he said.

Maeve suddenly felt an irresistible urge to annoy him. 'Can Bianca and Steph come with me?'

'No!' he shouted, pointing towards the music storeroom door. 'Go, now, this instant!'

At recess, Maeve, Steph and Bianca took up their position on the bench under the jacaranda. 'You shouldn't wind up McCabe,' said Steph. 'He's cool. I mean, he's not like a regular teacher. I heard he used to be a famous musician or something and he only got into teaching to sort of discover new talent.'

'You're hopeful,' said Maeve, laughing.

'I heard he used to be a priest,' added Bianca. 'And that he chucked it in and ran off with one of his parishioners.'

'That's just gossip,' said Steph.

'I don't know. He's kind of handsome,' said Bianca. 'For

an old guy,' she added hurriedly. 'Like one of those twentieth-century movie stars. You know, like Harrison Ford.'

'I guess he's okay,' said Maeve. 'At least he sees us for what we are. All for one and one for all, hey?' She put her hand out and Steph and Bianca slapped their hands on top.

Shortly before the lunch break, McCabe came into the classroom and spoke to their maths teacher. They both glanced in Maeve's direction as they talked. Maeve felt a tight feeling in the pit of her stomach. He couldn't still be angry with her, could he? But he didn't look pissed off. Maeve couldn't read his expression at all.

'Maeve, Mrs Spinelli wants to see you in her office,' he said.

Maeve felt uneasy as the music teacher walked silently beside her all the way to the Vice-Principal's office. It wasn't until she was alone with Mrs Spinelli that she understood why. Mrs Spinelli came out from behind her desk and rested one hand on Maeve's arm. Maeve felt her heart start to beat faster. This was seriously weird.

'Maeve, sit down please, dear. I have some bad news. There's been an accident. Your mother's car was involved in a crash in the Cahill Expressway tunnel early this morning.'

Maeve felt her stomach hollow out. 'Mum? An accident?'

'Now, she's all right. She's in St Vincent's Hospital, but they haven't been able to get in contact with your stepfather and they need to find him.'

'He was going up to the Blue Mountains on a job,

I think. I don't know where he is. He's not answering his mobile?'

'Apparently not.'

'Ned, what about Ned? My little brother. She was taking him to crèche this morning. He was in the car.'

'I don't know, Maeve. I'm sure they would have said something about your brother if he'd been involved.'

Maeve remembered the story of a baby who'd been left under the seat when the family car had crashed. What if they hadn't realised Ned was in the car too? She felt dizzy. She put one hand on Mrs Spinelli's desk, to steady herself.

'I'm sure your mother is going to be all right, but is there anyone else who can go to the hospital in your stepfather's place? Is there a relative or a friend who you'd like us to contact? Your grandparents?'

'They're too far away. They live in Queensland. We don't have any family in Sydney. I have to go. I have to go to the hospital,' said Maeve. 'I have to be with Mum.'

'I don't know if that's appropriate, Maeve.'

'Please, Mrs Spinelli. I have to be near her. Even if Andy comes, I have to be there too.'

'You can't go to the hospital alone, Maeve, and you need parental permission to leave the school.'

'But my parent is at the hospital. And I wouldn't have to go alone. Steph and Bianca can come with me. Steph's mum, she's friends with my mum. She'll give permission. *Please*, Mrs Spinelli.'

Mrs Spinelli frowned and rubbed her forehead. 'I'll see what I can do.'

Five minutes later, Stephanie and Bianca were sitting either side of Maeve in the corridor.

'Mum's going to meet us at the hospital, Maeve,' said Steph. 'It will be okay. It will be okay,' she repeated, squeezing Maeve's arm. But Maeve was already starting to feel numb all over.

Mrs Spinelli came hurrying down the corridor towards them with McCabe beside her.

'Girls, Mr McCabe is going to drive you to the hospital where you'll meet with Stephanie's mother. She's coming from the northern beaches but won't be far behind you.'

When they got into the school car park, Maeve wanted to run to McCabe's car, but she forced herself to simply walk swiftly.

'Do you mind if we sit in the back seat together, sir?' asked Steph, putting her arm around Maeve protectively.

'Of course not,' said McCabe. 'Don't worry, Maeve. We'll be there in no time. Things always seem worse while you're waiting to confront them.'

7

The black chasm

McCabe was wrong. Maeve felt her knees grow weak as they walked up the steps of the hospital, as if she were walking into a dark tunnel. As the doors parted and they walked into the foyer of the hospital, she could feel a shudder run through Steph's body. A momentary panic surged through Maeve. She turned to Bianca but all the colour had drained out of Bianca's face and her eyes were glassy. She looked as frightened as Maeve felt. As if he knew they were falling apart, McCabe stepped in front of them and leant down to look directly into Maeve's face.

'Hang in there, Maeve,' he said quietly. 'You can do this.'

Then he herded the three of them gently towards the front desk. Maeve could barely understand the words he was speaking as the nurse looked from them to him.

'Oh God, Steph,' said Maeve. 'It's bad. I can feel it. I can feel this is really bad.'

'It'll be okay,' said Steph. But her voice was thin and frightened and Maeve could tell she didn't believe it.

McCabe guided them into a small waiting room with brown, vinyl-covered furniture and a picture of a sunset on the wall. Maeve found herself thinking it was a crap picture. Her mother could draw better than that. Her mother, her mother.

'I want to see my mum,' said Maeve. 'I want to see her now. Why do we have to wait?'

'C'mon, Maeve,' said Steph, taking Maeve by the hand. Bianca took her other hand and between them they tried to draw her over to one of the couches but she shook herself free. She didn't want to sit on the horrible vinyl furniture. If she sat down, they'd make her wait. Hospitals always made people wait, didn't they?

'She's still in Emergency,' said McCabe. 'When your stepfather arrives, they'll let him in to see her and then maybe you can go too.'

'But I'm her daughter. I've known her longer than Andy. I've known her all my life. He's only known her for three years. That's nothing.'

'It's the way it is, Maeve. He's an adult.'

'Mr McCabe, I'm not a baby. I'm fourteen in March. I want to be with my mother.'

McCabe's hazel eyes were steady and calm. Not like the nurses, who wouldn't meet her gaze. Even Steph and Bianca were staring at the ground, as if they couldn't bear to face what lay ahead.

'Sit with Stephanie and Bianca. I'll talk to the doctor.'

Steph began rocking back and forth very slightly as she hunched over on the couch. Bianca sat with her hands on her knees, her eyes blank, staring at the ugly landscape painting.

'Your mum will be okay. Your mum will be okay. They can do amazing things these days. They save people.'

Maeve looked at her crossly. 'Please don't, Bunka. You don't know yet. Let's just be quiet, and . . . and wait.'

On the coffee table in the middle of the room, there was a stack of women's magazines. Princess Diana stared out from the cover and Maeve had that tight, sick feeling again. Then she realised both her friends were looking at it and thinking the same thought. They hadn't been able to save Princess Diana. She'd been famous and rich and beautiful, but they hadn't been able to save her.

Maeve couldn't tear her eyes away from the picture. That was such a big story. She remembered the magazines plastered with Princess Diana's face all through her primary-school years. Maeve didn't want to be part of a big story. She wanted everything to be ordinary and the same. She didn't want any of this to be happening. She shut her eyes. Suddenly, she thought of the ouija board and the exploding glass. This wasn't a dream she wanted to come true. This was a nightmare.

Steph's mum, Julie, arrived wearing the same frightened expression as Steph, her gaze flickering around the room, from one girl to the next. Maeve couldn't bear to look at her either. Even when Julie hugged her, Maeve kept her eyes down. But when McCabe walked back into the waiting room with another man, Maeve stared hard into his face, trying to read him. If she kept looking at him, somehow all of this would start making sense.

'Maeve,' said McCabe, 'this is Doctor Wilson. He's been treating your mother.'

Maeve glanced at the doctor. He was a short, wiry man whose face was drawn with tiredness.

'I'm very sorry, Maeve,' he said. 'Your mother has

sustained extensive head injuries. I'd wanted to wait until your father arrived before . . .'

'He's my stepfather. You can talk to me. I need to know too.'

'Is there anyone else in your family that you would like to contact?'

'No, there's only me and my mum, so tell me now,' said Maeve, struggling to keep her voice even.

The doctor looked at McCabe and Julie, as if he couldn't bear to speak to Maeve directly.

'We have Ms Kwong on life support, but I'm very sorry to have to tell you that we won't be able to revive her.'

'What do you mean?' said Maeve, aware her voice was too loud, almost a shout.

'I'm very sorry, Maeve, but your mother is brain-dead. Do you understand what that means?'

'She's in a coma?'

'No, it's not a coma. There's no possibility of her recovering.'

Maeve bit her lip until salty blood filled her mouth. Steph and Bianca took a step towards her, each clutching the other's hand. Maeve felt light-headed, as if she might float away. The only thing that kept her tethered to the earth was McCabe's steady gaze, as if he was willing her to be strong.

'Can I see her?' she asked.

The doctor glanced across at McCabe, who simply nodded in reply.

'Very well.'

Julie stepped forward. 'I'll come with you, honey.'

'No, just Mr McCabe, please. I just want Mr McCabe

to go with me,' said Maeve, making her voice as calm as she could. 'Thank you.'

A nurse walked Maeve and McCabe to a lift at the end of a long corridor and they went up three floors. They followed the nurse for what seemed like miles until they finally came to a small alcove outside a room and Maeve knew they had arrived.

Maeve had never felt so frightened. What if her mother looked crushed and unrecognisable? How would she bear it? But then a wild, crazy thought came to her. Maybe if Sue heard her speak, heard her own daughter's voice, she'd wake up. Maybe the doctor was wrong. When Maeve said her name, she'd call her back, back from the other side.

The room seemed so quiet. There was no sound from the rest of the hospital, just the low hum of the machines that her mother was connected to. Sue looked tiny, like a small child adrift in the hospital bed. Her head was swathed in a turban of white bandages and there was a darkening shadow of bruises on one side of her neck. Her face was pale, as if all the golden hue had drained out of it and already she had become a ghost. A wisp of black hair lay against her cheekbone. Maeve wanted to touch her, to tuck the stray hair to one side, but suddenly was frozen, unable to move closer.

'I'm here, Maeve,' said McCabe, as if he'd seen her falter. 'I won't leave you.'

Maeve took a step nearer to the bed. Her mother's hand was resting on the bedspread. A long, thin tube was snaking up to a machine full of clear fluid.

'Why are all these machines on?' asked Maeve.

'We're waiting for your stepfather,' said the nurse.

Maeve felt a sob choke in her throat. She stepped forward and gently laid her hands on Sue's bare arm. She leant down and pressed her cheek against her mother's. She wasn't cold, she was warm, and Maeve could hear air moving in and out of her lungs. Surely the doctor was wrong.

'Mum,' she whispered, close to where the bandages covered Sue's ear. 'I'm here, Mum. It's me, Maeve. Please, Mum. Come back, Mum. Come back to me.'

But Sue lay utterly still. There was not a flicker of expression on her pale face. Maeve picked up her mother's hand, small in her own. The nails were clipped short, the way she always kept them so she wouldn't risk snaring any fabric. Maeve cupped Sue's hand gently between her own and traced the length of her mother's fingers, trying to feel the firmness of her mother's grip as their fingers enmeshed. That's how she knew she was already dead. It didn't matter that Sue's blood was still moving, that these machines were making her body keep breathing. Maeve knew she wasn't there any longer. Her mother was gone. The room was empty. Sue was never this still, not even in sleep. She was always so alive, as if a fire burnt inside her that made her shimmer with warmth and energy. And now the fire was out.

Maeve stood up and turned to McCabe.

'She's not there,' said Maeve, her voice small with bewilderment.

'That's only her shell, Maeve, but her spirit is still with us.'

'No, that's gone too. She's not here.'

'Would you like to pray, Maeve? I'll pray with you. It might help.'

Maeve shook her head. Though she went to chapel along with all the other girls at St Philomena's, prayer had never meant anything to her. Sue hadn't believed in any God stuff and neither did Maeve. The only thing that she had been sure of was that her mother would always be there for her.

Maeve sat on a chair beside the bed and pressed her face against the mattress.

'I want to wait here. I want to wait here until the end.'

People came in and out of the room and Maeve heard them murmuring quietly. She didn't bother to look up. It was only when two trembling hands rested on her shoulder that she opened her eyes. It was Andy. She got to her feet and they exchanged a quick, anxious hug.

'It's okay. I'm here now and Ned's all right,' he said. 'He was at crèche. He's fine.' He spoke slowly, as if to reassure himself as much as Maeve.

Maeve felt a knot of rage form in her throat, so tight she had to choke the words out. 'I know Ned's fine, but Mum's dead. Mum's dead.'

'Maeve,' he said. And then he was crying like a baby, the way Ned cried, as if the tears would never stop.

'What are we going to do without her?' he said.

Maeve looked at her mother's hand, still and small on the white hospital blanket.

'Without her,' she echoed. The future opened up like a black chasm.

8

Echoes and angels

The folding bed creaked as Maeve rolled over and Ned gave a whimpering sigh in his sleep. Maeve had given up her bedroom to Andy's parents, Nanny and Pa, who had come down from their home in Lismore to help look after Ned. Andy had suggested that Maeve might want to sleep in the living room but she liked sleeping in with Ned. If she woke up during the night she could listen to the soft snuffle of his breath and somehow feel safer than she felt anywhere else.

She lay watching Ned as he drew the satin edge of his blanket up close to his face and rubbed the silky fabric against his upper lip. When he opened his eyes and saw her, he smiled. 'May-Yay,' he said, his voice soft with sleep. He stretched his arms out through the bars of the cot and Maeve touched his fingertips, tickling the palm of his hand until he giggled and pulled it away. She lifted him out of the cot and took him into her bed, feeling the softness of his breath against her as she cuddled him. She drew the covers over their heads and pulled the bedside lamp in as a prop. When the two of them lay safely snuggled in the warm, pink glow of their blanket tent, everything felt normal. It was as if nothing had changed. Any minute, Sue would call for them to come down for breakfast. Any moment, they'd wake up and find their old life had come back and everything that had happened in the past week had been a bad dream.

Suddenly, the sheets and blankets were ripped away.

'Aren't you going to be late for school?' asked Andy tersely.

'I don't know. Maybe I won't go after all,' said Maeve.

'Oh yes you will,' he replied. Maeve sighed and got out of bed. As soon as she stood up, her shoulders sagging with misery, he relented. 'I'm sorry, Maeve. Maybe you should wait until after the funeral.'

'No, it's okay. I know we agreed I'd go today and I want to go, really. It's just hard getting started.'

'I know what you mean,' said Andy, his eyes brimming with tears again. Maeve thrust Ned into his arms and turned away. She didn't want to see him cry. She was tired of tears. She just wanted the funeral to be over, for everything to be finished with. But when she thought about the future, there wasn't an end to the next phase – life without her mother. It stretched unimaginably into the weeks and months and years ahead, like a dark road winding through fog.

At the breakfast table, she kept expecting Sue to step out from behind the pantry door and shout peek-a-boo. As if she'd been hiding, as if it had all been a game that everyone had taken too seriously. Andy came downstairs with Ned on his hip. Ned was making that new, whingeing, grumbly sound that he'd only just invented and trying to bite Andy on the shoulder.

'Hey, cut that out,' said Andy crossly, holding Ned away from him.

'He wants Mum,' said Maeve.

'I know that,' said Andy. 'But I'm all he's got from now on.'

'And me,' thought Maeve. 'He's got me.' But she didn't say it out loud. She was quickly learning that words didn't work the way they should when people were grieving, as if everyone heard things differently and misunderstood everything she was trying to tell them.

The phone rang constantly, but now neither Maeve nor Andy bothered to answer it. The hallway filled with echoes as the answering machine clicked into action, Sue's voice saying, 'You have phoned Sue, Andy, Maeve and Ned. Please leave a message after the tone.' Nanny would race to the phone to try and stop the machine, disturbed to hear her dead daughter-in-law's voice echoing through the house, but Maeve knew Andy felt the same as she did. They couldn't bear to think of changing the message.

People kept arriving at the house too, with flowers, with gifts, with food. It was so hard answering the door to people who didn't know what to say or how to say it, and she grew tired of having to thank them all the time. The kitchen quickly grew cluttered with boxes of Danish pastries, muffins and quiches, but Maeve couldn't eat any of it. When Nanny and Pa had finally arrived, they'd cleared the benches and set about putting some order in the kitchen. Maeve knew it was good that someone was looking after the practical things, that someone was making sure there was food for Ned. But she had to fight down her constant irritation with them too. When Nanny started clearing out the fridge, reaching to throw away a jar of old jam, Maeve had to run from the kitchen. She wanted to shout, 'But my mum made that jam, my mum made that jam and now you're throwing it away.' It was as if there were two voices in her head all the time, the normal one and another voice that was crazy and irrational with misery.

When Julie came to pick Maeve up for school, Maeve climbed into the back seat beside Steph and hugged her. Maybe now she could have one almost normal day.

'Thanks for this, Julie.'

'Oh Maeve, it's nothing. Nothing at all. You're so brave, going to school the day before the funeral.'

Maeve knew she wasn't being brave. She was running away. She just wanted to pretend that nothing had happened.

But from the minute she walked through the school gate, Maeve realised this was going to be one of the longest days of her life. Nobody knew what to say to her. Girls she thought were her friends seemed to step wide when they walked past her, as if she was a pile of broken glass in the middle of the corridor, as if grief was a disease that they might catch. Even Steph and Bianca kept looking at her with that wide-eyed, miserable expression that made her want to squirm. She knew they were devastated, but she didn't want to hear them talk about it.

They sat on the grass during lunchtime, just the three of them, an invisible force-field around them that no one else was willing to cross.

'Can you two lighten up a little?' said Maeve, tearing up a blade of grass and carefully shredding it. 'Just say something.'

Bianca and Steph looked at each other and winced. 'We don't want to say the wrong thing,' said Steph.

'I don't care what you say. Say anything. I need you to stay the same, guys. Be like you always are. Everything is changing so fast. Home feels – weird. Andy is weird. Everyone is weird. Andy's mum keeps saying he has to keep his fighting spirit. As if he ever had any. He couldn't fight his way out of a paper bag. And now he just walks around and cries more than Ned.'

'It's good your granny can take care of things for a while. I guess that's something.'

'She's not my granny. She's Ned's granny. My granny and grandpa are flying down from Queensland tomorrow but they won't stay with us. They'll stay in their flat in Potts Point. They have this place that they keep for when they come to Sydney. They never come to our house.'

'Wow, they must be rich.'

Maeve shrugged. 'Yeah, I guess, maybe. They live in Surfers and travel around a lot, but they're going to stay in Sydney until everything is sorted out.'

'But the funeral's all set, isn't it? What else is there to sort out?' asked Bianca.

Maeve couldn't answer for a moment. 'Me. They have to sort out what's going to happen to me.'

'What do you mean? You're not going anywhere, are you?' asked Steph, alarmed.

Maeve lay back in the grass and folded her arms across her face. 'I don't know. It's not like Andy is my real dad. He's only my stepdad, he didn't adopt me. I heard Nanny saying it was too much for him to raise two kids on his own. And I bet you she didn't mean he should send Ned away. Mum didn't have a will, so no one knows where I'm meant to go. Andy says it's up to Por Por and Goong

Goong, 'cause they'll wind up being my legal guardians.'

'Who?'

'My granny and grandpa. My mum's parents. That's their Chinese names for grandparents. They're okay. But I don't really know them all that well. I don't want to think about it. It makes me want to run away. Except I don't know where to run to.'

Steph and Bianca looked at each other. 'Don't you dare,' said Steph.

'You're not going anywhere,' said Bianca. 'Not without us.'

Something soft and ticklish hit Maeve on the forehead. She uncovered her eyes and stared up at her two best friends. With the sun behind them, Bianca's blonde hair and Steph's red curls made haloes around their laughing faces. It almost looked as though they were angels.

'All for one and one for all,' they chanted together as they scattered handfuls of fallen jacaranda blossoms over Maeve.

9

Dark waters

Maeve woke early on the day of the funeral. Ned lay beside her, curled up against her body like a sleeping possum. When he'd woken during the night and cried for their mother, she'd taken him into bed with her and he'd quickly settled back to sleep. She brushed his cheek with a kiss and slipped out of bed.

Out on the back verandah, the morning air was cool against her skin. A magpie sitting in the tall, stringy gum tree near the back fence sang to the rising sun. Maeve listened to the bird's call resounding across the garden. The day was bright and clear. It seemed all wrong. She shut her eyes, wishing that the sky would cloud over, that the day would become black and grey to match her mood.

Bianca and Steph came by in the morning. Their parents had given them the day off school so they could be there for Maeve. Ned was having a tantrum when they arrived. They came into Ned's bedroom to find the wriggling toddler pinned to Maeve's lap as she tried to dress him in his new white suit.

'Hey, monster,' said Bianca, poking Ned in the tummy.

Ned bared his small teeth at her and growled.

'Oooh, I am so scared,' said Bianca, putting her hands to her cheeks and feigning horror. Ned giggled and then growled again.

Bianca and Steph took one foot each and strapped Ned's new sandals on while Maeve buttoned up his jacket. Ned grew even more excited by the attention and started trying to press big, sloppy wet kisses on their hands.

'You are turning into a demon toddler, that's for sure,' said Maeve as she carried Ned into the kitchen and settled him in his playpen with a pile of toys.

Nanny and Pa were busy setting out plates of food for the wake and all the girls were set to work unpacking the boxes of hired crockery stacked around the room.

'Your mum's funeral is going to be so awesome, Maeve,' said Bianca, as she lined up cups and saucer. 'I bet there'll be a million people. She has so many friends. This will be the most amazing funeral ever.'

'Have you been to any other funerals?' asked Maeve.

Bianca blushed. 'No, but I can't imagine that . . . you know . . . an event or tribute or party or whatever will be better than this.'

'It's not a party,' said Steph.

'God, Steph. Undermine me, why don't you. I'm trying to be positive. Trust me, Maeve, it's going to be amazing, okay?'

'Yeah, well, I hope so,' said Maeve. 'I've never been to a funeral before either, but things aren't shaping up great, so far. Andy wanted Mum to be in her favourite red top but Por Por, my granny, she phoned last night and asked what Mum would be wearing and when he told her, Por Por started wailing down the phone and saying you can't dress her in red or she'll turn into a ghost. Andy looked like he wanted to faint.'

'She was probably just really upset,' said Steph.

'I know that,' said Maeve. 'But I've got this feeling we're doing everything wrong. Andy keeps asking me what Por Por is talking about and I feel really stupid, like Mum should have told me about all the Chinese traditions. But she never did. I mean, I know more French words than I do Chinese and I don't know anything about what you're meant to do at a funeral.'

'It'll be okay once they get here,' said Bianca.

Maeve put her hands over her face. 'I hope so. The thing is, they've never been here before. I mean, for the wake, that will be the first time they've really been inside this house. They never visit us here. We always have to meet them at a restaurant in the city or at their flat and Andy never comes along. What if I have to live with them? What am I going to do?'

Steph put her arms around Maeve. 'Hey, you're going to be okay. Just do one thing at a time.'

'Yeah,' said Bianca. 'Good policy. I've been trying to get something happening with Josh and with Omar and I've decided one boy at a time is a much better idea.'

'You can be such an airhead,' said Steph, reaching out and drawing Bianca into a group hug.

Maeve was standing in the hall in her new white sundress, holding Ned on her hip, when her grandparents arrived. The minute the door was opened, Maeve knew something was wrong. Goong Goong winced when he saw his grandchildren. Por Por stared at Maeve and then quickly turned to Goong Goong and started speaking rapidly in Chinese. Andy was trying to greet them but it was as if he were invisible. Maeve set Ned down on the floor and he pelted towards the kitchen, calling for Nanny at the top of his voice.

The noise broke the spell that had fallen on everyone standing at the threshold. Por Por was dressed in a white silk skirt and jacket. She turned to Andy and took both his hands in hers and mumbled something about it being a difficult time for all of them. Goong Goong stood staring out into the street, his long face etched with disapproval. He was dressed in a silvery-grey suit that almost matched the colour of his hair. Even though Maeve never knew what to say to her grandfather, she had always admired his quiet dignity. But today, there was something icy in his expression, something that made her dread having to greet him. Unconsciously, she took a step back into the darkness of the hall, wishing she could run away like Ned.

Por Por stretched her arms out to Maeve. 'Siu Siu,' she called, her voice cracking with grief.

Maeve had been taller than her grandmother since she was eleven years old, but it still felt strange to have to bend over to hug her. Por Por stroked Maeve's hair and held her close, just the way Sue used to, and Maeve felt a little catch in her throat. She hugged Por Por tighter and pressed her face against the smooth, silky jacket.

'I'm sorry we couldn't come sooner, sweetie,' whispered Por Por. 'We're here for you now. We'll always be here for you.'

Maeve fought back tears. She took a step towards her grandfather. 'Goong Goong,' she said, standing on her tiptoes to kiss him on the cheek.

Goong Goong simply nodded. Maeve wasn't sure if it was because he was upset that they were all still standing outside. She looked to Andy and gestured with her eyebrows, hoping he'd take the hint.

'Oh, would you like to come in for a cuppa? We're still getting organised but you're very welcome,' he said, awkwardly.

Por Por smiled but shook her head. 'No, we won't interrupt. We just wanted to see the children before the funeral. But I'm sure you've got much more to organise. Maeve, if you and Ned get dressed, we could take you to the church with us.'

'I am dressed, Por Por,' said Maeve.

Goong Goong frowned even more severely and Por Por pursed her lips. 'But shouldn't you be wearing black?'

Maeve glared at Andy. He had told her that she and Ned should both wear white because it was a Chinese tradition. Suddenly her new dress felt tight and uncomfortable. 'But you're in white, Por Por,' said Maeve.

'Isn't white the Chinese colour for mourning?' asked Andy.

'For adults. Very disrespectful for children to wear white at the funeral of their mother,' said Goong Goong, turning away and walking towards the gate.

Por Por reached out and grasped Maeve's hands. 'He's very upset, sweetie. It's too much, too sudden. We'll wait in the car for you. Come out with Ned when you're ready.'

'But Por Por, I've got my friends with me. I'm going to the funeral with my friends.'

'And Ned is coming with me,' said Andy. When Por Por turned to answer him, he cut her off before she could speak. 'He has to go in his car seat. He's too little to ride in a regular seatbelt. It's not safe. He's coming with me.'

Maeve tried to ignore the angry undertone in Andy's voice.

'It's okay, Por Por. We'll all be together at the funeral.' She squeezed Por Por's hands to reassure her and fought down the tears that were still trying to work their way free.

Steph and Bianca flanked Maeve on either side like bodyguards as they walked into the church together. There were so many people that Maeve hardly knew, spilling out of the aisles of the church, crowding in at the doorway, and everyone was staring at her. She'd never been so glad of her friends.

A pair of Buddhist monks stood near a small Chinese altar, chanting prayers and lighting incense while the minister of the church greeted mourners at the door. A picture of Sue sat on the coffin amid wreaths of flowers. Shyly, Maeve approached it and placed the card that she had made beside Sue's photo. Inside was a print of Ned's small, chubby hand and Maeve's long, slender one surrounded by a pattern of interwoven hearts. Briefly, her fingers touched the lid of the coffin. It was as if an electric shock charged through her and left her cold and trembling, to know that her mother was inside that box. It was a relief to sit down between Steph and Bianca and feel their warmth.

Por Por had arranged the Buddhist monks but Andy had picked the church. Maeve had never been inside it before.

A song called 'Forever Young' was playing in the background as more and more people crowded into the church. She caught sight of some students from St Philomena's standing with McCabe and Mrs Spinelli at the back and wished she was standing among them, that this was somebody else's funeral, anybody but her mother's.

Andy spoke, in a broken voice about how happy he and Sue had been together and the home they had made. Maeve felt all her energy tunnelling towards him, willing him to keep talking, praying that he wouldn't break down and cry. If Andy fell apart, then she probably would too. The effort of simply keeping it together made her feel as if she couldn't breathe, as if she was riding a wave of tears that at any moment would overwhelm her. Sensing she was unravelling, Steph and Bianca put their arms around her, holding her in a group hug that fused the three friends together. Even though they were crying too, even though their tears were warm against her shoulder, Maeve knew they would keep her from drowning in the dark ocean of her grief.

10

A bridge of magpies

As Maeve walked through the front door, she saw Goong Goong standing in a corner of the living room, clutching a cup of tea. It was the first time she'd ever seen him inside the house. She knew she should go up and speak to him but she felt suddenly angry. Why hadn't he ever come inside when Sue was alive? It was too late now. She pushed her way along the hall, keeping her gaze down.

All around her, people were talking about her mother. Every room was crammed with friends and distant relatives that Maeve didn't even know she had, glancing at her with pathetic expressions. She didn't want to see all these people smiling at her nervously and saying extra-nice things about her mother. She wanted to be alone, to shut her eyes and shut out everyone and everything. She hurried past the kitchen where Steph and Bianca were helping Nanny with the food, out through the back door, under the thick overhang of bougainvillea and down the timber stairs. She heard Ned calling her name from somewhere inside but she couldn't stop. Suddenly, overwhelmingly, she needed to hide.

The key to Sue's studio was hidden under the fifth potplant on the windowsill. Quickly, Maeve turned it in the lock and pushed the door open, making sure she shut it tight behind her. No one had been in Sue's studio since the accident. Maeve could only think of it as 'the accident'. Somehow it seemed less final, as if an accident was a small thing and not the huge and crushing event that had smashed Maeve's world to pieces.

In the mornings Sue's studio was full of light, but now that it was late afternoon, shadows crept across the high fanlight windows. The concrete floor was cool beneath her as she sat behind a stack of silk screens. All around her, shelves were piled high with bolts of hand-painted fabric. A huge mesh shawl with a pair of knitting needles sticking out from amidst the silvery yarn dangled over the edge of one of the workbenches. Maeve pulled a handful of the shining fabric over her head. It fell gently like a waterfall across her shoulders and gathered in shimmering folds around her.

It felt safe in the studio. She loved the sweet, oily scent of her mother's paints, the linty odour of the bolts of fabric, the sharp bite of the inks that Sue had used to print her designs. Maeve felt her heartbeat slow, her breathing become steady again. She wrapped the shawl tight around her and pressed it to her cheeks. Everything in the studio had a different meaning to her now. Everything in it seemed fragile and precious.

On the floor beside her, tucked away underneath the workbench on a low shelf, was a pile of old journals, their wiry black spines threaded with cobweb. Maeve bent down and blew some of the dust away, ran her finger along the cold metal. She knew the sketchbooks were full of her mother's drawings and ideas. One by one, she pulled them from the shelf and flipped through the pages. They were crammed full of designs and notes on different projects.

At the very bottom of the pile was a small book with a green cover. She prised it out from under the heavy black folios and ran her fingers over the silky fabric binding. It was older than the other journals and only a few pages had been used. Sue's name and student number were written in bold letters on the inside cover. Opposite was a sketch of a girl weaving clouds and below her a tiny figure of a man and an ox. A wide river of stars flowed between them. On the next page Sue had written half a page of notes in English about someone called Weaving Girl and carefully drawn some Chinese characters alongside the English words. Magpies flew between the notes and along the edge of the page, meeting to form a small bridge that arched across the third page of the book. Then nothing else.

Maeve flipped through to the end. Tucked into the very last page was a photo of Sue holding a tiny baby. At first Maeve thought it might be Ned that her mother cradled so gently, but when she looked closer, she realised it was herself. She turned it over, and there in her mother's handwriting were the date and the words, *'My little warrior princess'*. She couldn't fight back the tears any longer. They rose up like a tidal wave, choking her until she was gasping for breath. Finally, she lay down exhausted, pressing her hot cheek against the cold concrete floor.

Maeve was still clutching the photo and the green journal when Por Por came into the studio. Instinctively, Maeve froze, not wanting to be discovered. She watched from her hiding place as Por Por walked around the room, touching the bolts of coloured fabrics, bending down and resting her face against a pile of half-finished lengths of painted cloth.

Maeve shut her eyes and tried to stay still, as still as a mouse, and not move. She felt Por Por's footsteps draw closer. Then she realised Por Por was crying, her breath coming in ragged gasps. Maeve lifted a corner of the silver fabric and gently touched her grandmother's knee.

'Por Por,' she said in a small voice. 'It's me.'

'Siu Siu! Little darling, what are you doing in here all alone?'

Por Por knelt down and took Maeve's face in her hands, wiping away tears with her thumbs.

'You and me, we both know the place to cry, don't we?' she said. She sat down on the floor beside Maeve and picked up a corner of the silver shawl. She didn't seem worried that her immaculate white skirt might get dusty. She brushed the shawl against her cheek, just as Maeve had, and her neatly coiffed black hair fell forward, hiding the sadness in her dark eyes.

'My Weaving Girl. I can't believe she's gone,' said Por Por.

'Weaving Girl?' asked Maeve. 'Mum drew a picture of her, I think.' She held out the notebook at the page showing the girl in the clouds.

Por Por touched it with her fingertips, tracing the outline of the floating girl, then she took the book and turned the pages, looking at the words and images hungrily. Finally, she sighed and gave it back to Maeve. 'She must have been just pregnant with you when she drew this. August, near the Chinese lovers' day. Like St Valentine's Day, but more romantic.'

'More romantic? What do the Chinese bits say?' asked Maeve.

'It says Milky Way Girl. The same as Weaving Girl. She wove clouds,' said Por Por, covering her eyes with one hand, as if the sight of the book had hurt her. 'In Chinese tradition, Weaving Girl was a goddess who fell in love with a mortal. He was a cowherd, a farmboy, and they had two children together. But Weaving Girl's grandmother, the Heavenly Mother, came and found her and took her back into the sky.'

'But why?' asked Maeve.

'Because Weaving Girl belonged in Heaven. The cowherd and his children, they tried to follow, but the Heavenly Mother made a swirling river that they couldn't cross.'

'That's so mean. She was taken away from her family for ever!'

'They were only separated. Every seven years, a bridge of magpies formed between Heaven and Earth and the cowherd and the children, a boy and a girl, crossed over to meet her.'

Maeve stared down at the picture. She tried to imagine a bridge that she and Ned could cross to get back to their mother.

'Was my dad – was he like the cowherd?'

Por Por grew very still. 'He wasn't the right man for Suzy. It wasn't like the story. None of us were gods. Your grandfather knew it wasn't going to work from the start.'

Maeve felt her insides grow hard. She shut the green book and held it against her chest.

'Goong Goong doesn't even care that Mum's gone,' she said angrily.

'Maeve! Don't say such a thing! Of course he cares,' replied Por Por. 'It's not his way to cry, to make a scene, but he is heartbroken, absolutely heartbroken.'

'He wanted Mum to be a boy. And because she wasn't a boy, she didn't matter. She couldn't worship the ancestors, or at least it didn't count. He thought me and Mum didn't count. Because we were girls, because she was an artist. I know all that. I heard Mum and Andy fighting about it.'

Maeve bit her lip to choke back the other angry words that were bubbling inside her and trying to escape.

'That man, that Andy!' said Por Por, almost spitting his name out as if it was a bad taste in her mouth. 'How can he say these things! He doesn't understand.'

Por Por put her arms around Maeve and gently stroked her hair, just the way Sue used to. 'It's so hard for your grandfather,' she said softly. 'Not like for you and me. Siu Siu, I'm like you. I grew up here in Australia, so I know you can have things of the old world and of the new. All your grandfather wanted was for Sue to belong to his world and his traditions. Is that so terrible? To be frightened of losing the child you love?'

'But he did lose her. Not because of the accident. He lost her even before I was born,' said Maeve, through hot tears.

'Then you mustn't let us lose you too,' said Por Por, holding Maeve close to her. 'Please, Maeve. You know we want you to come and live with us. When I was a little girl, I lost my mother too. She was sent back to China and I stayed in Australia with my grandmother. It felt terrible at first, but my grandmother, I loved her so much, she made a good life for me. Please Maeve, let me make a good life for you too.'

Maeve couldn't stop the tears from streaming down her face. Warrior princesses weren't meant to be so pathetic, but she couldn't help herself. The longer Por Por hugged her, the more the strength drained out of her body until she felt she was melting in her grandmother's arms.

'It's okay, little one,' whispered Por Por. 'Don't cry. Goong Goong and I will take care of you. Everything will be all right. No one will keep you from us now.'

11

Hell to pay

It was cool inside the skyscraper and Maeve was glad to be out of the heat. Por Por led the way up an escalator to the restaurant on the first floor. The waiters in black and the crisp white tablecloths immediately signalled that Goong Goong's favourite restaurant was way fancier than anything Maeve had ever been to with Andy and Sue. Goong Goong was sitting at a table near the window, keying something into a palm pilot, and he barely glanced at them as they joined him. Outside the window, the giant arc of the glass was patterned with an intricate mosaic, and an ornate clock counted off the minutes. Goong Goong began talking in Chinese to Por Por in a low, exasperated tone. Maeve studied the mosaic. It reminded her of the one all around the stove at home, how Sue had carefully laid one piece at a time in place until the blue and green pattern rippled like a river. She quickly averted her gaze, trying to steer her thoughts away to stop the memory overwhelming her.

The first round of dumplings arrived swiftly and her grandparents fell silent, intent on the serious business of eating. Maeve didn't know what to choose. Sue had always ordered dishes that she knew Maeve would like – soft, sticky rice wrapped inside a lotus leaf and sweet egg custard buns that let out a puff of steam when you cut them open. But now there were all kinds of weird things arriving on little plates or inside bamboo steamers – marinated chicken feet, squid covered in chilli and squiggly plates of beef stomach covered in black pepper. Maeve poked at what she hoped was a pork dumpling, peeling off the translucent skin and examining the filling. She stared at the pale meat inside and suddenly wasn't hungry any more. The hands of the clock outside the window ticked over.

'Siu Siu, *siu sum*,' said Goong Goong. '*M'ho wan sic mut.*'

Maeve started and looked at her grandfather questioningly.

Slowly, as if speaking to a little child, Por Por said, 'He told you to pay attention and not to play with your food.'

'How can I pay attention when you won't speak any English?' replied Maeve, fighting down an impulse to shout.

'How will you ever learn to speak Chinese if you don't hear it spoken?' snapped Goong Goong.

Maeve stared at the napkin in her lap. She folded it up into the tiniest paper boat and watched it sailing across the fabric of her skirt.

'Siu Siu, sweetie,' said Por Por. 'Once you start to understand Chinese, we'll take you to Hong Kong with us, remember?'

Maeve stared down at her plate. Her mother hadn't said anything about having to know Chinese to visit Hong Kong. But then her mother hadn't needed to introduce her to a bunch of relatives who might disapprove of her.

'You'd like that, wouldn't you, Maeve?' asked Por Por.

Goong Goong spoke sharply to Por Por in Chinese. Even though Maeve didn't understand all the words, she knew what they were fighting about. It was the same old thing. Goong Goong thought her mother should have given her a proper Chinese name, not a crazy Irish one. Maeve had never once heard Goong Goong call her by her real name, always Siu Siu which she knew just meant 'little'. 'Little, little', that's how much he thought of her feelings.

'I don't want to go to Hong Kong. I just want to go home,' whispered Maeve.

'You don't feel well? You want to go back to the flat?' asked Por Por, her voice suddenly soft and full of tenderness.

'No, I mean back to Balmain. I want to go back to my own bedroom in my own house.'

'Your home is with us now. We have decided to sell that old house. The money will be put in trust for you and Ned, for when you're older.'

'But what about Andy? That's his home too! I don't want you to sell it.'

'That house was never in your mother's name. It belonged to us. We will help Andy find something smaller, something for him and Ned.'

Ned. She hadn't seen Ned for two whole weeks, the two longest weeks of her life. They'd never been apart like this before. Just the mention of his name made Maeve want to cry. 'I want to go back and live in *my home* with Ned. With my family.'

'We are your family, Siu Siu. You can't live with that

man. He's not your father,' said Goong Goong, his voice heavy with disapproval.

'He's Ned's father, and Ned's my brother,' replied Maeve. She could tell her voice was too loud. People at the other tables were turning around to stare. Her grandparents laid down their chopsticks and looked at Maeve, their faces full of alarm.

'If we could, we'd bring Ned to live with us too, but that man would never allow it,' said Goong Goong, lowering his voice to an angry whisper.

'Stop calling him "that man"! He has a name. He's called Andy,' said Maeve.

'You see. You don't call him your father,' said Por Por, looking from Goong Goong to Maeve, caught between their fury.

'I don't call anybody "father",' said Maeve, turning on her grandmother. 'I don't have a father. You drove him away. You made Mum break off with him, just like in that story. You were just as horrible as the Heavenly Mother. You didn't even want me to be born! You wanted Mum to get rid of me!'

Por Por put one hand up to her face, as if warding off a blow. Maeve wanted to scream at her, *If it wasn't for you, Mum would still be alive*, even though she knew it didn't make sense. She threw her serviette onto the table and ran out of the restaurant, jumping three steps at a time down the escalator to the ground floor.

By the time Maeve reached Circular Quay, she was breathing hard. Her halter top was drenched in sweat and she tugged at her short skirt with annoyance. She felt uncomfortable inside her own skin. When her mobile rang, she put it on Silent. She knew it was Por Por trying to call but no way was she going to answer. She was sick of being sensible. Of trying to be good. Of trying to make everyone else feel everything was okay when it wasn't.

Maeve sat alone in the bow of the ferry as it chugged across to Balmain in the morning sunshine. Little flecks of white crested the water as it struck against the sides of the ferry and the fresh harbour breeze made her feel calmer. She pressed a hand against her chest and felt the dull thud of her heartbeat against her palm.

Maeve knew her parents had met on a ferry. Sue had told her how a man with black hair and pale blue eyes wouldn't stop staring at her. And then he'd come and sat beside her and unfolded a map of Sydney and asked for directions. Maeve shut her eyes and tried to imagine her mother as a student, sitting beside the handsome young Irishman. She spun her iPod to the old song that her mother had always joked was about her father, 'Love Will Tear Us Apart'.

Maeve reached into her bag and drew out the silky green notebook. She'd carried it with her every day since the funeral, studying the pictures of Weaving Girl and the cowherd, wondering if the man in the drawing looked anything like her father, wishing her mother had written more.

Every day, she'd tried to write something about her mother in the green notebook, as if it would somehow make Sue's story live longer. But the words wouldn't come. Only images. She drew a heart surrounded by black knives and then, almost without thinking, began sketching faces behind the dark heart. Faces of ghosts, with their weeping, angry eyes, and their tiny mouths full of sharp teeth. When she'd finished, she put everything back into her bag. She couldn't think about the dead any more. She needed to be with the living.

Taking a short cut up a narrow laneway littered with purple jacaranda petals, Maeve ran up the hill from the wharf. The doorbell echoed through the house and then she heard Andy's voice, a loud whisper, calling down from the balcony above.

'Hey, Maeve! We were just having a morning nap, me and the kid. We had a rough night. You let yourself in. I'll be right down.'

Maeve turned her key in the lock. She hadn't been back to the house since the day after the funeral two weeks earlier. Andy came down the stairs in rumpled clothes, wiping the sleep away from his eyes. He gave Maeve a quick hug and then stepped back and looked at her. 'I reckon you've grown, even in just a couple of weeks!'

'No I haven't,' replied Maeve, smiling. It was so good to hear Andy's dorky voice again. 'Can I tiptoe up and see Ned? I won't wake him.'

'That's okay. You can wake him up. I'll never get him to sleep tonight if he doesn't get up soon. You go get him and I'll put the kettle on for a cuppa.'

Ned was asleep on the double bed, his arms flung wide. Maeve stood watching him for a moment and then she smoothed his silky brown hair away from his forehead. He opened his eyes and stared at her, heavy-lidded. But when the light of recognition dawned on his face, he pulled away and rolled over to the other side of the bed.

'Ned, it's me, Maeve,' she said, attempting to draw him towards her. She tried to kiss his palms, but he kept his fists shut tight and scrunched his face up, as if he were going to cry.

'Ned?' she said, bewildered. 'What's wrong?'

Ned narrowed his eyes and made a low, growly noise in the back of his throat. When she tried to kiss his cheek, he reached up and scratched her hard across the face. 'No!' he cried out, at the top of his voice. Maeve touched the skin on her forehead where it was stinging.

'Bad, Ned,' she said, her lip trembling.

'Go way,' he replied crossly. Turning his back on her, he pulled the sheet up over his head and sat on the far side of the double bed.

Maeve flung herself on the mattress, burying her face in the bedclothes, and burst into tears.

'Ned,' she said, his name coming out as a broken sob. 'Ned.'

Maeve heard Andy calling from downstairs but still she wept. Then she felt Ned clamber towards her until his face was so close to hers she could feel his warm breath against her skin. Very gently, he touched her tears with his fingertips. Maeve opened her eyes and saw that tears were trickling down his cheeks as well.

'I miss you, Ned,' she said. 'I didn't want to go away.'

'No go way, May,' said Ned, suddenly wrapping his arms tight around her neck and squeezing until she could hardly breathe.

She held him tight, inhaling the sweet smell of him.

By the time she carried Ned down to the kitchen he was laughing and trying to lick her face. She used to hate it when he pulled that cheeky trick but now it only made her giggle.

'He missed you,' said Andy.

'I missed him too,' said Maeve. 'I want to come home, Andy.'

Andy took a step back, his cheeks suffusing with colour. 'It's not up to me, kiddo. I'm not your legal guardian. It's up to your grandparents.'

'Well, you have to tell them that you want me to be with Ned. That Ned needs me.' She framed the sentences carefully so he wouldn't have to say he didn't want her.

'Look, Maeve, your grandparents . . . They have bags of dosh. I don't. And I don't have any legal rights over you.'

'But that singer, Bob Geldof, he got custody of his ex-wife's daughter.'

'I'm not exactly a rock star, Maeve. I can barely keep body and soul together as it is. I can't afford to take your grandparents to court. By the way, do they know you're here?'

Maeve settled Ned in his highchair and hung her head, avoiding Andy's gaze.

'Don't they know you're here?' he repeated, louder. He ran both hands through his hair. 'Jesus, kiddo. You're just making things harder for all of us.'

Suddenly, Maeve realised how exhausted he looked. She glanced around the kitchen. The sink was full of dishes, the compost bucket was full to overflowing and a crowd of small insects buzzed around a bowl of rotting grapes.

'I can help. If I come home, then I can help with things and clean and do stuff and be with Ned. I don't need looking after.'

'Maeve! Things are bad enough without you stirring up trouble. You can't waltz in here without your grandparents' permission. I just want to keep the peace with them, okay.'

'You shouldn't be scared of them, you're a grown-up.'

'For Christ's sake! It's got nothing to do with being scared. They'll think I put you up to this and then there'll be hell to pay. I'm gonna call them, right now.'

'No, Andy, don't!' But he was already in the hall, dialling. Ned stopped trying to climb out of his highchair and stared at Maeve, his face crumpled with alarm. He looked at Andy and then back to Maeve before letting out a piercing scream that made the windows rattle. Maeve covered her ears and ran down the hallway, into the hot sunshine.

12

Runestones

It was a relief to be in the street. When she'd run two blocks and was standing in the cover of a café entrance, she pulled out her mobile. There were three missed calls from her grandmother's phone. She was glad Por Por didn't know how to send a proper message. She deleted the calls and dialled Bianca.

'Hey, Bunka,' said Maeve, her voice shaky. 'It's me. Where are you?'

'Oh, hey Maeve, I'm . . . kind of busy. Can I call you back?'

'I need to see you, like now.'

'Ummm, do you want to come to the footy?'

'What? I can't hear you. What's all the shouting?'

'I'm in Randwick. Josh and Omar are playing footy. Omar says he's going to take me out for coffee after the game.'

'Bianca, I need to talk to you this afternoon.'

'I can't hear you. You're breaking up.'

Suddenly the line went dead. Maeve knew Bianca had hung up. Quickly, she texted Steph: *B @ home. Everything sux. Coming over. M.*

An unexpected shower of rain washed Darling Street clean and left the air sticky with humidity. Maeve turned into Steph's street with relief. Going to the Maguires' house was almost like going home. She could always count on Steph. When Julie hugged her as soon as she opened the door, Maeve wanted to hold on, to keep her face pressed against Julie's shoulder. She wasn't her mum but she was somebody's mum and it made Maeve miss Sue even more.

Inside, the kitchen smelt sweet and safe and familiar. There was a big pile of choc-chip cookies on the kitchen bench and Steph was munching on one while she turned the pages of an oversized book.

'You're just in time,' she said. Beside her plate of cookies lay a purple velvet bag and when Maeve sat down beside her, Steph picked it up and shook it gently.

'Runes,' she said, putting on her mysterious, wise-woman expression. 'Bianca's mum gave them to me as a special present. A sort-of "becoming a woman" present.'

Maeve laughed. It felt so good to be acting as if nothing had happened. To be talking to Steph as if it was just any ordinary sort of day. She had thought that the minute she saw Steph she'd want to pour her heart out, but to be able to pretend that nothing had changed was even better. 'Bianca would have loved that,' she teased.

'You know what Serena's like – a bit of a hippy but a really nice hippy. She gave Bianca heaps of presents when she got her first period but Bunka thought it was embarrassing. I wasn't embarrassed. I think it's cool. Serena says I can use the runes to help solve problems. You can sort of get answers to questions with them.'

'I so have a heap of questions I need answers to.' Maeve

reached out to stroke the purple velvet but Steph pulled the bag away. 'No, only the owner of the runes can use them. I had to do all these rituals to make them soak up my energy. But I can do a divination for you, if you like.'

Maeve ate another chocolate cookie. Her mobile phone was vibrating in her bag but she ignored it and took a second cookie in her other hand so she could take bites from both.

'You have to ask a question in the right way,' said Steph. Then you get the right sort of answer.'

Maeve licked the chocolate off her fingers slowly. There were so many questions. Should she fight to stay with Andy? Should she make peace with her grandparents? Why had her mother died so young? Where was her real father? Her eyes started to fill with tears.

'Let's go up to my room,' said Steph. 'We have to have the right setting.'

Steph's bedroom wasn't much bigger than a cupboard and they reached it by climbing up a long stepladder. The room was built into the roof of the house and the walls sloped in crazy directions. Steph threw two cushions on the floor beside her bed and then made Maeve sit down.

'Okay. Shoot. What's up?'

Maeve gave a crooked half-smile and then told Steph about the events of the morning. When Maeve reached the part where Ned scratched her face, Steph let out a little groan and reached for Maeve's hand.

'So I don't know what to do,' said Maeve.

'That's big,' said Steph. 'That is so big, Maeve.' For a long moment they sat in silence, staring at the purple velvet bag. 'We could ask the runes,' said Steph.

Maeve laughed grimly. 'It wasn't exactly the sort of advice I was looking for.'

'You could ask something like, I wish the rune to comment on the issue of where I should live.' Steph picked up the bag, shook it gently and held it in her hands with her eyes closed, as if for a moment she were praying. Then she opened the bag and offered it to Maeve. 'Okay, choose a rune.'

Maeve shut her eyes. The stones clinked together softly as she rummaged among them.

'Take one,' said Steph.

Maeve held the small stone in her hand and stared at it. It had two lines in the simple shape of a sideways 'V'. Steph leaned forward and looked at it, then she reached for her book.

'I think that one's called *ken* or *kenaz*. Yeah, here it is, it's the sixth rune. It means knowledge. It's meant to be the symbol of a flaming torch.'

'It doesn't look much like a flame. It just looks like a squiggle,' said Maeve, feeling a little disappointed.

Steph scanned the page. 'It says that it's about enlightenment. That you've got to find enlightenment.'

'I know that,' said Maeve. 'I want to know what the answer is, though.'

'Well, I guess it means you have to look inside yourself. Sort of seek wisdom inside or something like that.'

Maeve groaned. 'That's a crap answer.'

Steph wriggled uncomfortably on her cushion. 'Maybe it would have been better if you'd got this one.' She peered into the purple bag and rustled around until she found the rune she wanted. 'It's called *rad*. It's like the symbol of the cartwheel – sort of about how everything turns and passes. You know, that you get over things.'

'What, you mean like my mother dying? You think I'll get over that?'

Steph blushed. 'I didn't say that.'

'It's easy for you to think, though. Your life goes on. You're in the same house with your mum and your dad and your brothers. But my life doesn't go on. My life is shit,' Maeve said.

'Maeve, I loved your mum too. If there's anything I could do to change things, I would.'

Maeve stood up and kicked the cushion into a corner. She sat down on the edge of the bed and put her head in her hands. For a long while, neither of them spoke. Stephanie kept glancing at her watch and frowning.

'Look, Maeve, I'd love to stay here with you and help but I have to go,' she mumbled.

'What?'

'I have to go to work. I'm babysitting the Atwell kids this afternoon.'

'I'll come with you,' said Maeve, desperate not to be alone.

'You can't. They're pretty uptight about strangers. Anyway, the kids are brats, you wouldn't enjoy it.'

'I'll wait here then, until you come back,' said Maeve, folding her arms across her chest.

'Maeve, why are you acting so weird?'

'Do you think,' said Maeve in a small voice, 'do you think maybe I could live here? Like, with you and your family?'

The silence seemed to stretch into a breathless, empty void.

Suddenly, they could both hear Julie calling.

'It's your grandmother, Maeve. Come and talk to her at once!'

Maeve could hear the disapproval in Julie's voice and knew that Por Por had told her all about Maeve having a hissy fit and storming out of the restaurant.

'I can't talk to her,' said Maeve. 'What am I going to do?'

'Take the back way out,' said Steph.

Above their heads was a skylight opening onto the corrugated iron roof. Steph pushed it upwards and boosted Maeve through. As Maeve slid down the ladder at the side of the house and jumped the fence into the street, she could hear Julie calling her name. She ran all the way down the hill to the quay, her head fuzzy with pain and confusion.

Once the ferry had chugged out into the harbour she began to feel calmer. She sat in the bow and the wind whipped her hair across her face. She raked her hands through it and pulled it into a ponytail, her fingers snagging in the friendship braid at the base of her neck. It brought back all her rage. What was the point of having friends if they couldn't help you out when you needed them most? She wanted to rip the braid from her scalp. Reaching into her bag, she found a pair of nail clippers and cut the matted plait away from the nape of her neck. It lay in her hand like a rat's tail, a curling, multi-coloured tangle of hair. She raised her arm to fling it into the swirling green waters of the harbour, but a sudden gust of wind made her lose her balance. Hard rain slapped her in the face. It ricocheted off the surface of the darkening harbour waters like bullets.

Maeve retreated inside, the braid still held tightly in her clenched fist.

She sat staring out at the driving rain. The clouds had turned inky black. It reminded her of a dream she'd had after the Bali bombings. The Harbour Bridge had blown up, Kirribilli was on fire, and plumes of smoke swirled above the Opera House. Maeve had been sleeping over at Bianca's house and was woken by Bianca and Steph shaking her out of her nightmare.

Maeve rubbed the braid between her fingers, feeling its rough texture. She took out her green notebook and slipped the multi-coloured tress between the pages.

For two hours Maeve stayed on the ferry as it circled Sydney Harbour, until the ticket lady told her the shift was changing and it was time to get off. As the ferry chugged towards Circular Quay, she gazed back at the lights of Balmain. Yurulbin Point glittered in the darkness. What were Andy and Ned doing right now? Maybe Ned was having a bath, surrounded by plastic floaties. Maybe Andy was cooking his weird enchiladas. Steph would be coming home from her job, Bianca would be sitting in a café with Omar.

As she stepped off the ferry, she couldn't believe that in all of Sydney she had nowhere else to go but back to her grandparents.

13

Out of the shadows

Night fell as she walked aimlessly across the Botanic Gardens, under the dark branches of the Moreton Bay fig trees. She couldn't go back to the flat in Potts Point. Not yet. Maybe never. When she finally reached Macleay Street, she headed towards Kings Cross, trying to put purpose in her stride, as if she actually knew where she was going.

Ahead of her flashed the lights of Darlinghurst Road. When she arrived at the junction where Macleay Street turned into the Cross, she came to a standstill, suddenly self-conscious. What did people do when they wanted to get away from everything? Putting her head down, she turned into a gloomy side street. A drunk lay asleep in one of the doorways, his filthy, crumpled coat pulled up to shield his face, his body reeking of sour alcohol. She'd always thought getting drunk was pathetic but suddenly she understood why someone might want to climb out of their body and abandon the whole world. She had to keep walking. If she stopped for even a moment, everything might come crashing back into her head. The night air felt thick, dark and oily around her. Suddenly she found herself in Victoria Street with St Vincent's

Hospital looming up ahead. As if compelled, she walked towards it.

At the entrance to the hospital she stood staring blankly, remembering. She could see herself walking up those steps with Steph and Bianca. She could see that moment when the doors swung open and the smell of the hospital hit them. It should have changed everything. But Steph and Bianca were the same people, worrying about their stupid boyfriends and their stupid jobs. As if everyone was simply meant to get on with their lives, as if nothing had happened. She clenched her fists and turned her back on the hospital.

At the William Street bridge, she hung over the railing and stared down at the traffic scooting into the tunnel. Car headlights hurtled beneath her, bright against the darkness. It made her shudder. She would never feel the same about cars again.

In the heart of the Cross, a crowd of laughing drunks spilled out of the doors of a pub where 'happy hour' was drawing to a close. One of them broke away from his friends and began to follow her. Maeve felt panic rise up in her throat. She quickly turned down one of the side streets and jumped into a doorway, pressing her back against the cool bricks, watching the man pass. When she was sure he was out of sight, she sat down on the doorstep and wrapped her arms around her knees.

On the other side of the street, two old men were sitting on the footpath, looking shadowy and forbidding in the harsh streetlight. Maeve wished she was invisible. When one of the men opposite stood up and looked as though he was going to cross over to talk to her, Maeve jumped to her feet.

'Maeve. Maeve Kwong!' he called. Maeve stared. It was McCabe.

'Sir?' she said, trying to hide her incredulity. Why was McCabe hanging out in a side street of the Cross? McCabe turned to say something to his companion and then waved for Maeve to join him.

As Maeve drew near, she could smell the other man. He stank of tobacco, alcohol and something acrid and unwashed. McCabe protected the flame of a lighter as his friend drew deeply on a skinny hand-rolled cigarette.

'And what brings you down to this part of town, Maeve? I don't expect to meet my students wandering around the back streets of Darlinghurst in the dark.'

Maeve was glad her face was in shadow so he couldn't see her blush. 'I was on my way to . . . to my grandparents.' She could see that he didn't believe her. He'd know that her grandparents would never allow her to wander around Kings Cross alone at night.

'Like Little Red Riding Hood,' said the grubby old man beside McCabe, cackling until his laughter turned into a hacking cough.

'Dibs,' said McCabe. 'This is one of my students. Maeve, Dibs McGinty. We were at school together.'

'Were we, mate?' asked Dibs. 'Was you at St Bart's or that other place? What *was* that other place? Damn my friggin' memory.'

McCabe put one hand on Dibs' shoulder. 'Clontarf *and* St Bart's. We've known each other a long time.'

Maeve felt creeped out by Dibs. A milky-white film covered his pale blue irises. Now that she was standing closer, she could see he had only one leg. The fabric of his right trouser was folded over his knee and held in place with safety pins. Leaning in the shadows of the wall was a crutch with a plastic shopping bag slung over it.

'Dibs and I were about to go and buy some fish and chips. I think you should come along, Maeve.'

For a split second, Maeve contemplated running away. McCabe watched her, as if he knew everything she was thinking, as if he sensed why she was wandering around alone. She knew he wouldn't let her out of his sight easily.

'Okay,' she said glumly.

Dibs swung himself up on to his leg, hooked the plastic bag over his free shoulder and tucked his crutch in place. They headed towards the flashing neon of Darlinghurst Road. Dibs refused to go into any of the cafés but Maeve suspected they wouldn't have welcomed him anyway. Now that they were in the bright lights, she could see how filthy he really was. Grimy wrists stuck out from beneath his old greatcoat and his fingernails were black with dirt.

McCabe bought them each a bucket of hot chips and a piece of fish and they walked back to the William Street overpass. On a wide set of steps outside a Chinese restaurant, Dibs lowered himself to the ground. Maeve made sure McCabe sat between her and the old drunk. Behind them a red neon sign glowed with the single word 'Confucius'. Before them lay the city at night – the Centrepoint tower, flashing neon signs in blue and red, and a Sportsgirl billboard with a giant girl stretched across its length. Maeve tried to keep her gaze fixed on the night skyline. Watching Dibs eat made her feel queasy. He held a chip between two grimy fingers and then licked the salt and oil from his fingertips.

When they had finished, McCabe gathered up the paper wrappings and gestured to Maeve to stand. 'You take care then, Dibs,' he said. 'Maeve and I have to get going. Don't we, Maeve?'

Maeve nodded. She watched as he slipped a twenty-dollar bill into Dibs' hand. Dibs shrugged as if it was his due.

As they walked away, Maeve couldn't help asking, 'Do you owe that man money, sir?'

McCabe smiled. 'No, but he needs that twenty dollars a lot more than I do.'

'Did he fight in a war or something? Is that how he lost his leg?'

'No. He was in an accident.'

Maeve shuddered. 'On the Cahill Expressway?' she asked. 'I hate that road. I hate it. Someone should blow it up.'

McCabe didn't answer straight away and Maeve knew she must have sounded crazy.

'Maeve, what are you doing wandering around the Cross alone on a Sunday night? Surely your grandparents or your stepfather must be wondering where you are?'

Maeve hung her head. A shiny metal plaque was set in the footpath beneath her feet. *'How RUTHLESS and HARD and VILE and RIGHT the young are.'* Hal Porter. It was horrible to think that someone thought that about her. That Goong Goong probably thought she was all those things.

'I can't go back to my grandparents, sir. I can't. They want me to come and live with them in Queensland. I want to stay here, in Sydney, but I can't because nobody wants me. My brain feels all squeezed up and my chest feels hollow inside, like someone's scraped out my heart and there's nothing but a big aching hole inside. What's wrong with me, sir?'

'There's nothing wrong with you, Maeve. You've lost your mother. You're in grief now, but things will change.'

'You mean I'll get over it,' said Maeve bitterly. She was so tired of people telling her that one day, a day she couldn't imagine, she'd accept her mother's death.

'No, you never get over losing your mother, but things change, whether you want them to or not.'

Maeve looked at McCabe, as if seeing him for the first time. Teachers weren't meant to sound like that. Teachers were meant to tell you to move on.

'I want my old life back,' she said quietly.

Across the road, a busker stood in the entrance to the Kings Cross subway. His song, an old Oasis song, echoed out into Darlinghurst Road. Maeve shut her eyes and felt the words inside her. *'Don't look back in anger, I heard her say . . .'*

'C'mon, Maeve,' said McCabe. 'I'll buy you a cool drink at the Fountain Café but then I'm taking you back to your grandparents.'

Maeve was ready to let go. All of a sudden, she felt too tired to stay angry. She trudged along beside McCabe, like a prisoner returning to her jail. At the Fountain Café, she sat slumped in a white plastic chair while he ordered them both an ice-cold glass of lemon squash. In front of them, mist from the thistle-shaped fountain shimmered in the night air.

'Cheer up, Maeve. Queensland could turn out to be great. You're about to begin a whole new life.'

'You mean live in the moment and forget the past,' said Maeve.

'No, I don't mean that. Your past is always with you. But moving to Queensland isn't the end of the world.'

'Sorry, sir,' she mumbled. 'But you don't get it.'

McCabe sighed and drummed his fingers on the white plastic tabletop. His face looked sharp and lonely in the silvery glow of the city lights. The wide canvas awnings rippled above them, making the shadows flicker. When McCabe leant towards her, Maeve thought he had the saddest expression she'd ever seen.

'Grief is a lonely place, Maeve. Nobody really "gets it". Nobody can go into that darkness with you. But you have to have faith that things will get better. I know that it's a terrible thing to lose your parents. I lost my parents too. Dibs and I, we were in an orphanage together, first in England and then in Western Australia. Not long after I left Clontarf, the boys' home in WA, Dibs went on an excursion. His bus overturned on a road south of Perth. That's how he lost his leg. Some boys died. Others lost both legs. I found Dibs again in the Cross about five years ago, and I knew that but for the grace of God it could have been me. But I was the lucky one. I was taken in by an old man who became like a grandfather to me. You can't know the future, Maeve, but you have to trust in it. You have people who love you. No matter how hard they are to get along with, you have to have faith in them and in yourself.'

Maeve stirred the straw in her glass around until the ice tinkled. She wanted to apologise for something but she wasn't sure why.

'How come no one knows that about you, sir? I mean, at school, people think you used to be a priest or a musician or something.'

McCabe laughed. 'You can tell your sources that I've been those things too. Everyone has secret lives, Maeve.' He pointed to his heart and then at Maeve, his silver hair falling forward as he leant towards her. 'Even now, you have so many secret lives inside you, Maeve Kwong. Your dreams, your hopes and fears – they're all part of the story you're making for yourself right now. One day you'll have so many stories to tell your grandkids. Just as your grandparents probably have amazing stories they could tell you.'

Maeve tried to imagine what untold stories her grandparents might be hiding. There were probably thousands that Goong Goong and Por Por had never shared with her. It made her feel both curious and uneasy thinking about it. 'But what if I hate living with them? What if Queensland sucks?' she asked.

'You might love it. You won't know until you try,' said McCabe, getting to his feet.

As they walked away from the café, a gust of warm night air rippled across the El Alamein fountain. Maeve held out her hands and shivered at the touch of the cool water on her bare skin. Something had changed. Something inside her had shifted.

'It's just down the road. You don't have to walk with me all the way,' she said, turning to McCabe.

'I think I do,' he replied.

'Don't you trust me?'

'It's not about you, Maeve. I don't trust who you might bump into.'

'That sounds like something my mum used to say.'

At the entrance to her grandparents' apartment building, McCabe turned to Maeve.

'Would you like me to come up with you?'

'No, please don't, sir. I need to do this alone. Besides, Goong Goong is all weird and formal around foreigners.'

'You mean me?'

'Yeah, well, I know you're Australian and we're in Australia, but for my grandfather, everyone who isn't Chinese is a foreigner.'

'I would like to meet your grandparents some time,' said McCabe. 'I'm sorry I didn't introduce myself at the funeral. I've often wondered if you were related to an old friend of mine.'

'Kwong is a pretty common name,' said Maeve, shrugging her shoulders. 'Most of my grandpa's family are still in China.'

McCabe watched her from the apartment entrance as she stepped into the lifts. She knew he'd stand guard until he was sure she was safely upstairs. She stared at her reflection in the mirrors. Her hair was full of wind and salt from riding the ferries all afternoon and there was a dark half-moon beneath each eye. She covered her face with her hands and was glad to hear the ping of the doors opening.

Por Por answered the door and Maeve could read every emotion on her grandmother's face; relief, anger, love and bewilderment were all there in equal measure. She threw her arms around Maeve, kissing her on the cheek and stroking her tangled hair. She smelt of tea and fried dumplings and Chanel No. 5 all mixed together in layers of warmth and sweetness. Maeve's eyes prickled with tears, but she bit her lip and fought them back.

Suddenly, Por Por fell silent and pushed Maeve away from her. Standing at the lift doors was Goong Goong, his car keys in his hand.

'Your grandfather has been driving all over Sydney, looking for you,' said Por Por.

'I'm sorry,' said Maeve. 'I'm sorry I made you worry. I won't do it again.'

'No, it will not happen again,' said Goong Goong. 'Nor will we speak of this incident.'

He strode into the apartment and slammed the door to his study.

'He was worried, sweetie,' said Por Por, as she ushered Maeve into her bedroom. 'But you're home now. Home where you belong.'

Maeve stood by the bedroom window, looking out at the twinkling lights of Woolloomooloo Bay. Her suitcase lay open on a chair next to the bed. A clock chimed midnight, its tone muffled as if a blanket of silence had fallen over the apartment. Maeve shut her eyes. She had to let go of the past and accept that next year she'd be at a new school with new friends in a new state. She had to try to make it work.

14

The first Christmas

Goong Goong's BMW was like an icy refrigerator. Outside, palm trees stood like sentinels along the roadside and the canals shimmered in the heat, but inside the car it was freezing. Maeve felt as though she was travelling across another planet in a weird ice bubble, not just another state. Everything looked strangely dry for the tropics and the grass along the verge was brown and crisp.

She pushed her iPod earphones tighter and focused on the beat of the music. She didn't want to think about the new school yet. McCabe had said that – don't worry about it until you've actually arrived. But everything was happening too quickly. Maeve hadn't even finished up the year at St Philomena's when Goong Goong and Por Por decided to bring her to Queensland. She didn't mind missing the end-of-year school events but it had been tough having to give up on the Christmas dance concert. Every time she thought of Steph and Bianca dancing without her, her heart skipped a beat. Now she was having to face not only dancing without them but spending the rest of her school life among strangers.

The driveway of Ingleside College seemed to go on

for ever. The buildings stood on a rise above playing fields where the grass lay green and spongy, and deep-set verandahs made the school look cool and inviting. But when Maeve opened the car door, the heat hit her like a fiery wall.

The school was nothing like St Philomena's. Maeve noticed how new everything was, from the wide, open walkways to the shiny surfaces in the classrooms. Even the chapel was modern, with a sharp, spiky tower and an abstract stained-glass window. As she followed Goong Goong and Por Por around, Maeve kept picturing the dark chapel and shady grounds of St Philomena's and all the places she and Steph and Bianca used to sit. There was nowhere to hide in this school, nowhere that friends could share their secrets. But maybe there wouldn't be anyone she'd want to confide in. She thought of Steph and Bianca with sharp longing.

They left the Vice-Principal's office with a thick shiny brochure that explained everything the school had to offer and a wad of pale green forms to fill out.

'You'll like this school, Maeve,' said Por Por. 'Much more than that old St Philomena's.'

'I loved St Philomena's,' said Maeve. Quietly, she took out her mobile and sent a text message to Bianca and Steph. *New school has boys but who cares? St Phils rocks. Miss u. M.*

Maeve woke with a start. For a moment she lay absolutely still in the dark, listening to her pounding heartbeat, so loud, so urgent, above the roar of the surf. She got out of bed and pushed the filmy curtains aside. Even though there was only a sliver of a moon, the cresting waves shone white in the darkness of the ocean.

She flicked on her bedside lamp and reached for the silky green notebook.

Secret Facts from the Secret life of Maeve Lee Kwong
On 12 September 2001, me and Mum were staying
at Surfers. We had the whole apartment to ourselves.
I was sneaky when I was a kid. I got out of bed at
dawn and tiptoed into the living room to watch MTV.
But when I turned on the telly, the World Trade Centre
was falling down. It was like a bad movie. I panicked.
What if planes everywhere started flying into tall
buildings? What if I had to jump out the window? We
were on the 16th floor! I started crying and Mum came
running into the living room, still in her pyjamas. When
she saw what I was watching, she started to cry too,
but she picked up the remote and turned off the TV.
She took my hand and led me out to the balcony.
I was freaking out but she made me follow her.
The ocean was pink and gold in the early morning light
and the air was sweet and clean. Mum told me take a
deep breath. We were alive and we were safe.
It feels like that happened in another life – my life
with Mum before Andy and Ned came along.
So the secret fact is if you look at the sunrise and
take a deep breath it helps you feel brave.

She went to the balcony to watch the sun inching its way over the horizon and took a very deep breath.

It was Christmas morning. Her first Christmas without her mother.

Goong Goong and Por Por weren't very interested in Christmas, so Maeve was surprised to see a huge box wrapped in pink paper and gold ribbon sitting on the coffee table in the living room. There was even a mini Christmas tree beside it. She wished it didn't remind her of the live pine tree that she and Sue had decorated together the year before. Goong Goong looked up from his newspaper and tried to smile as Por Por raced out of the kitchen.

'Happy Christmas, Siu Siu,' said Por Por, kissing Maeve on the cheek.

Maeve gave her a hug back and then knelt down beside the coffee table, staring at the present.

'Aren't you going to open it?' asked Goong Goong.

Slowly, Maeve peeled away the layers of wrapping paper.

'Wow!' she said, when the last piece of pink paper lay on the floor beside the box. 'My own laptop! Cool! Thanks.'

'And there's a connection in your room with broad-band so you can send those email things to your friends whenever you want,' added Por Por, looking to Goong Goong as if to affirm that 'email' was the right word to use.

Maeve stared at the laptop. She knew Por Por was unhappy about how much time she'd been spending in the Internet café at the end of the street. Now she'd have no excuses to leave the apartment.

'Would you like me to assist you in setting it up?' asked Goong Goong, folding his newspaper neatly.

'Thanks, Goong Goong, but I can figure it out.'

She picked up the silvery laptop in one hand and carried the box with all the accompanying computer cords in the other. In her room, she quickly worked out how to get the laptop running. In Sydney she'd always had to argue with Andy or Sue to get any time on the family computer. It gave her a weird feeling to open all the different applications and license them to herself. As soon as she'd worked out how to get the computer connected, she logged onto MSN as Warrior Princess Kicks Arse. No one else was online. Why would any of her friends be sitting at a computer on Christmas morning?

She was scrolling through some of her old messages when the computer peeped to let her know another person had come online.

It was someone called 'Dancing Man'. Maeve frowned. Who the hell was Dancing Man? She checked his profile and then remembered that Bianca had met him in a chatroom and insisted everyone had to include him on their MSN. Maeve looked at his message and wondered if she should ignore it.

Hey 's'up, WPKA?

Maeve hesitated before responding.

Asl?

14mSYD – U?

13fQLD.

Hey, Merry Xmas! What'd u get?

A laptop. U?

A mobile – but my baby bro hammered it and it's broke already.

Crap.

My bad – I let him hold it. He's cool.

Maeve imagined Ned on her knee, playing with her new laptop. She wouldn't want him to break it, but she would so love to have him around. This was probably his best Christmas yet and she'd missed it. His first Christmas, he'd been too little to appreciate any of it and Maeve had unwrapped all his presents. Last year he was only getting the hang of it, and this year should have been perfect. She tried not to think of all the fun she could have had with him. Suddenly, the new laptop lost its appeal and Dancing Man didn't interest her.

Gtg. Cya she signed off.

If only she could hear the sound of Ned's voice, maybe Christmas wouldn't feel so depressing. She listened for the sound of her grandparents in the next room. She knew they were in the living room but the apartment was as quiet as a chapel. She went out on the balcony and put her iPod on, spinning to a song by Ashley Ballard called 'Don't Get Lost in the Crowd'.

Slowly she started to dance, in smooth, melancholy movements. It felt like a good song for her mood. But when Ballard sang about 'finding your own voice' Maeve turned off the music. She stood on the balcony listening to the sound of the surf breaking on the white beach. From far away came the sound of a child laughing. More sharply than ever, Maeve knew her old life was lost. She drew a deep breath.

15

Kingfisher Creek

On Boxing Day morning, Por Por was up early.

'Quickly, Siu Siu,' she said. 'We have to be in Brisbane for when the department stores open.'

Maeve sat up in bed and rubbed her eyes sleepily. 'Why?'

'The sales! The Boxing Day sales, silly girl,' said Por Por.

Maeve had never met anyone who knew how to shop like Por Por. It was like an adventure, a sport, a fantastic sort of game where the aim was to get the most beautiful objects or clothes for as little money as possible. Por Por always found the best things for the tiniest prices.

Por Por turned onto the freeway and put her foot to the floor. Maeve caught her breath. Goong Goong drove with such measured patience, it was always a shock getting into the car when Por Por was behind the wheel.

'Aren't you speeding a bit, Por Por?' asked Maeve, watching the speedometer needle tip past 120.

Por Por sighed and eased off the accelerator a little. 'Mrs Annie Mahoney, the woman who taught me to drive, she had no patience for speed limits. If she were alive today, she'd think it's crazy we have these beautiful roads and have to drive so slowly on them.'

'I never want to learn to drive,' said Maeve, looking out the window at the landscape flashing past. 'Not after what happened to Mum.'

Maeve could feel the mood inside the car shift. 'Perhaps you'll feel differently when you're older,' Por Por said quietly.

They drove in silence for the rest of the trip. Maeve hadn't meant to make Por Por sad. There were so many unspoken rules between them, rules about what they could talk about and what subjects were taboo. Talking about Sue was definitely a topic that was too hard for Por Por to handle. Sometimes Maeve felt exhausted trying to navigate her way through the complicated maze of silences.

Maeve and Por Por returned from their shopping spree late in the afternoon, laden with bags of new clothes. Goong Goong was standing by the door, waiting for them. He tapped his watch impatiently. He had a flight to catch and needed Por Por to drive him to the airport at Coolangatta.

Maeve took Por Por's bags and let herself into the apartment, excited to have it all to herself. She put a CD of her favourite dance songs into the stereo and turned the sound up high. As soon as she heard George's 'Breathe in Now,' her mood lifted. This is what she'd been missing, music that filled the room and hummed through the floor. She pushed the furniture out of the middle of the living room and made a space big enough to dance in, big enough for her to stretch every muscle.

Even though she swam every day in the apartment

swimming pool, her body felt stiff after weeks away from dance class.

When Santana's 'Just Feel Better' swelled near its finish, Maeve felt a surge of energy, an extra charge in her movements. She didn't mean to kick so high. She didn't mean to catch the edge of the dragon plinth with her foot. The timing couldn't have been worse. As the dragon slid forward, Por Por opened the door of the apartment, just in time to watch her favourite ornament tumble onto the parquetry floor and smash into pieces. Maeve ran to the stereo and hit the Off button.

'Oh Por Por, I'm so sorry. I was only dancing,' she said, kneeling to gather up the fragments.

Por Por stood staring down at the shards of broken porcelain, her face stiff, her eyes glazed. 'It's not important,' she said.

She walked past Maeve and sat down on the sofa.

'When is all this going to stop? It's one blow after another.'

'I'm really sorry, Por Por. I didn't mean to break it,' said Maeve.

'No, Siu Siu. It's not you. There's been a disaster. A tidal wave, a tsunami,' said Por Por. 'It will be on the news by now. It's swept away thousands of homes and lives. At the airport, it was chaos. They were cancelling flights, people stranded, their plans all changed. I said to your Goong Goong, I said, stay, but he went to Singapore and left me alone.'

'You're not alone,' said Maeve. 'I'm here, Por Por.'

Maeve sat beside her grandmother, holding her hand as they watched the news. Por Por seemed to be shrinking into the pale yellow sofa. The lists of countries affected grew longer. Maeve put her arms around Por Por and hugged her tight.

'You're a good girl, Siu Siu,' said her grandmother, patting Maeve on the hand. But Maeve could see that Por Por was far away, thinking of people she knew in South-East Asia, thinking of other times and wishing that Goong Goong was with her.

Maeve felt guilty but she couldn't wait to escape the apartment. Knowing that Bianca and her mother were going to take her down to Byron on New Year's Day was the only thing that had made the quiet night in the apartment bearable. She'd already packed her bag, folding her T-shirts, rolling up her jeans and tucking her spare bathers into the side pockets of her dance bag days in advance. Por Por had wanted to buy her a new suitcase, but Maeve liked her beat-up old bag, even if the zip was stubborn and the fabric worn and raggedy.

On the morning of her departure, Por Por was grumpy. She banged pots around in the kitchen and pretended to find fault with everything from the texture of the *congee* to the fact that Maeve didn't want to eat it. Por Por always had *congee* for breakfast, white rice porridge with a sprinkling of fresh spring onions and crunchy fried shallots on the top. Maeve was too excited to eat more than tea and toast. She dipped her spoon into the honey pot and then into her teacup, watching the gold liquid melt into the pale green tea. After breakfast, she sat on the carved ornamental chair in the hallway, her hands folded in her lap, quietly waiting while Por Por padded around the apartment, complaining that the cleaner hadn't dusted her collection of jade ornaments, that the house plants were looking weedy and that she really wasn't in the mood to have her friends around to play mah jong that evening. Maeve knew it was all because Por Por didn't want her to go.

At 10.30 Bianca pushed the intercom in the foyer. Maeve grabbed her bag and raced to the door.

'Aren't you going to invite them up for tea?' asked Por Por. 'They've driven all that way. They'll want a cup of tea.'

'I'll put my bag in their car and ask them,' said Maeve.

'Don't be silly, Maeve.' Por Por pushed the buzzer and spoke into the intercom. 'There. They'll be right up.'

Maeve glared at her grandmother. She knew that Por Por wanted to check out Bianca's mother to find an excuse to keep her prisoner in the apartment the whole of the summer. She was just working herself up for a good argument when the doorbell rang. Por Por opened the door and then suddenly, there was Bianca. And Steph!

'Steph! I didn't know you were coming too. When did you get here?' She threw her arms around both her girlfriends. It was so good to have someone her own size to hug.

'They picked me up from the airport on the way here. I couldn't let you two live it up in Byron without me!' said Steph.

Bianca's mother Serena followed the girls into the flat. Maeve worried that she was looking particularly boho in layers of floaty blue Indian cotton and long strands of coppery beads. Her thick brown hair was streaked with blonde highlights and her scarf had little bells along its edge that tinkled as she crossed the living room. Maeve glanced at her grandmother anxiously. It would be a disaster if Por Por decided Serena was 'unsuitable' – she might change her mind about letting Maeve go. But Por Por treated Serena like a long-lost friend, insisting she sit on the sofa and enjoy a cup of her best green tea.

Once Maeve realised that Serena was safe, she dragged Steph and Bianca into her bedroom.

'I can't believe you're here,' she said, as Steph and Bianca looked around her room. 'I've missed you guys so much.'

'Can we help you pack?' asked Bianca, sliding open the big mirrored wardrobe and eyeing Maeve's clothes hungrily.

'You mean can you borrow something,' said Maeve, laughing.

'It's been a total drag since you left. Steph's gear – well, you know it doesn't add a lot of pizzazz to the communal wardrobe.'

Steph rolled her eyes and walked over to the window to look out at the ocean. 'Great view,' she said. 'Do you like living here?'

Maeve picked up her dance bag. 'I don't want to talk about it now,' she said, lowering her voice. 'I'll tell you later.'

Outside in the street, a mud-splattered four-wheel-drive stood waiting for them. Maeve flung her bag in through the back door beside Steph's huge blue suitcase, which probably held enough clothes to last the whole summer.

'It's not all mine,' said Steph, catching Maeve's expression. 'I had to bring up emergency supplies for Bunka.'

Once they were off the freeway, flat fields quickly gave way to folds of hills as they climbed into the hinterland behind Byron Bay.

'You are so going to love Kingfisher Creek,' said Bianca. 'That's where we're going to stay. My uncle owns it but he's overseas. It's paradise.'

They turned up a steep, muddy track and drove higher into the misty hills.

'Wow, it's like something out of *The Lord of the Rings*,' said Steph, putting her face against the window. 'You can almost see Elijah Wood stepping out from between the trees.'

Maeve looked out at the thick, green forest. It *was* like something out of a fantasy novel. Vines hung from huge trees, birds flitted in and out of the dense, lush undergrowth. Serena parked the car outside a sprawling timber house and Bianca jumped out first, putting one hand forward for each of her friends.

'All for one and one for all, guys. The Three Musketeers together again, at last!'

16

Written on the hand

Maeve, Steph and Bianca stretched out on their mattresses and stared at the rain. They each had unrolled their bedding on the polished wooden floor of the guest bungalow. There wasn't much furniture in the room but the long French doors opening onto the garden and the high cathedral ceilings made the room feel like a private temple.

'I can't believe our bad luck,' said Bianca. 'It's never rained here before.'

Maeve laughed. 'Of course it rains here. How else did it get to be so tropical-looking?'

'Yeah, I know. But not when I'm on holidays. Not when I'm in Byron. It never rains then. I wanted for us to go surfing and get great tans before we go back. It's all right for you. You can walk across the road any time and you're at that big beach at Surfers – full of spunkrats.'

'I don't think so!' said Maeve. 'My grandmother won't let me go to the beach by myself. She thinks someone will kidnap me or a tsunami will drown me. I just hang around by the pool. And I don't really want a great tan, anyway. I get all these freckles.' She touched her nose and looked at it, going cross-eyed with the effort.

'Your freckles are cute. Asian chicks with freckles look authentic. Not like me,' said Bianca. 'If I had freckles, I'd just look – I don't know – spotty.'

'I'm not Asian. I'm Aussie.'

'Whatever,' said Bianca. 'I just wish this rain would stop.'

'I don't mind the rain,' said Steph. 'This place is like heaven, even if it is raining. I love it, Bunka. And your mum is such a great cook too. Lunch was fantastic. I think I want to be a vegetarian too.'

'Don't encourage her,' said Bianca. 'She'll do the full hippy thing on us and we'll wind up eating lentils and tofu and all that weird vego stuff every night.'

Maeve sat up and shrugged. 'Hey, my granny cooks tofu all the time. And I like lentils way better than chicken feet, which is what Por Por would cook for you if you stayed with us. So chill. Steph's right, this place is paradise. Look at this room. It's like a dance studio or a party venue.'

'I know!' shouted Bianca. 'I know just what we should do.' She jumped up and dragged her mattress over to the wall, clearing the floor. 'Kingfisher Creek Dance School is about to rock 'n' roll.' She flipped through her CD wallet and put a disc in the portable player on the floor. 'C'mon, Musketeers. Time to 'Lose Control' with Missy Elliott. You missed this one, Maeve. Louise got us working on it the week after you went up to Surfers. It's serious hip-hop. You'll love it.'

It only took a couple of run-throughs for Maeve to perfect the moves. Sliding into the finale she could feel a rush of adrenalin. Then, finished with hip-hop, they moved on to their anthem, the Thunderbugs' 'Friends Forever'. They leapt and spun, using every inch of floor space in the bungalow. Maeve felt sweat trickling down her back and wanted to shout with happiness. Bianca and Steph looked into her eyes and, as if they read her mind, they laughed before shouting the chorus, 'We'll be, you'll see, we'll be friends forever!'

They were working their way through a jazz piece when Serena came running across from the main house under the cover of a big blue golf umbrella.

'Just like the three Graces,' she said, as she opened the doors of the bungalow. 'I thought you lot might be sick of being inside. What do you think about an excursion?'

'Mum, you're scheming. I know that look.'

Serena smiled. 'Steph and Maeve will love it, darling. You know they will.'

'Not Crystal Castle!' exclaimed Bianca.

Serena ignored her and turned to the others. 'Pop your sandals on, girls. We'll go in about five minutes, okay?'

'What's Crystal Castle?' asked Maeve, after Serena had hurried back to the main house.

'It's this sort of hippy place with crystals and fortune-telling and stuff like that,' said Bianca.

'Sounds cool,' said Steph.

Bianca tipped her head to one side and gave Steph a sly look. 'You and Mum have already talked about this, haven't you? I swear, she should be your mother, not mine! Just remember, we're not going to do any more magic crap. Not after what happened with the ouija board.'

'You just won't give it a chance. Magic stuff can be fun!' said Steph, pushing a handful of curly hair away from her face.

'Look, you don't like Omar. I don't like fortune-telling.'

'Do you really not want to go?' asked Maeve.

'It's okay. Someone's got to play with Mum or she'll get lonely. At least it's somewhere to shop!'

Steph laughed and Maeve looked from one friend to the other. Something had happened between Steph and Bianca while she was away, as if not having Maeve to sort out their differences had forced them to grow even closer. It made her dread having to go back to Queensland without them. Janet Jackson's song 'Together Again' was playing in the background as they sat in a circle, strapping on their sandals. Maeve shut her eyes for a moment and made a silent wish that they could stay together forever.

They drove to Mullumbimby through thick, lush forest. The man selling tickets at the entrance to Crystal Castle wore a green velvet cloak. When Steph told him he looked like a real wizard, he flung back the cloak with a dramatic gesture and winked at her. Bianca had a hard time fighting down a snicker but Steph blushed scarlet.

'C'mon,' she said, grabbing Bianca and Maeve by the hand. 'Serena said the gardens have a really magic feel about them.'

'You were going to say "vibe",' said Bianca.

'No I wasn't,' snapped Steph.

Maeve linked her arms through both of theirs. It was good to be between them again, to think they might still need her, connecting them. They came to a pond with an elegant Indian sculpture standing serenely in the centre. The sound of frogs croaking was so loud Steph covered her ears.

'I can't see any frogs,' said Bianca, as they drew closer to the pond. 'I bet they have a tape playing behind those reeds.'

'You are such a cynic,' said Steph.

'That's why you're so lucky I'm your friend. You need me, Steph, or you'd be swallowing all this mumbo-jumbo wholesale.'

Maeve steered her friends along the winding paths and into the first gallery, where there was an exhibition of Mardi Gras–style costumes. The girls moved among the models, exclaiming at the intricacies of the needlework. Maeve couldn't help thinking that her mother would have loved the designs. She made a mental note to draw one of the outfits in the green notebook that night.

Inside the main building, sunlight cut through a glass display case of crystals and created rainbow prisms of light on the floor. Wind chimes tinkled and the air was heavy with incense. Bianca headed straight to the jewellery display, but Steph had other plans.

'Hey, look,' she said, 'you can get your aura photographed here!'

Serena came up behind them. 'Why don't you get one each, girls? My treat.'

A young woman explained that they had to sit in a chair that was especially designed for aura photography and keep their hands on the metal arms.

'You get to choose a complimentary crystal too,' said the photographer, offering them a basket of smooth, polished stones.

Bianca picked a stripy golden-brown stone, Steph took pale pink and Maeve selected a shimmering yellow crystal flecked with silver. It felt cool and magical in her palm.

'That's citrine,' said the photographer. 'It's a survivor's stone, it gives you courage when the chips are down.'

Maeve smiled. 'What do the other ones mean?'

'The pink stone, that's rose quartz. It's a symbol of unconditional love. It opens your heart.'

'Lurve,' said Bianca. 'Romance, it's all going to happen to you this year, Steph. I can feel it. How about my stone?' She held out her crystal.

'That's tiger's eye. It's really good for flighty people and kids with ADD. It's calming.'

Steph laughed and Bianca looked a little put out. 'Well, it's got a cool name and I like the look of it. I don't care what it means.'

When the prints were ready, the girls crowded in close to see. A cloud of colours swirled around each figure. Steph was surrounded by purple and green, Bianca by blue and pink, but Maeve's aura burnt fiery red with a single blaze of white just above her head.

'Looks like I'm burning up,' said Maeve.

'Well, red is good. It means happiness, doesn't it?' said Steph. 'That's what it means in China, anyway. So that means you're destined for happiness.'

The girl at the counter smiled. 'Colours have different meanings in aura photography. Red is a powerful symbol of anger and energy. And I think that white bit means a spirit is watching over you.'

'Like a guardian angel?' asked Maeve.

'Something like that,' said the girl. 'But look, I've only just started learning about auras so I can only give you a general idea. The fortune-tellers can give you a better explanation.'

'I think I'm over all this future crap,' said Bianca. 'I need to get into the moment and buy something.'

'I want to see the fortune-teller,' said Maeve impulsively.

'Oh no!' said Bianca. 'Mum will be stoked. She'll think she's won you over too!'

'My granny gave me some spending money. I may as well spend it on something.'

'You'd rather spend it on a fortune-teller than on clothes? And I guess me and Steph can try on all the goddess clothing,' said Bianca. 'I could look amazing in green velvet.'

Steph groaned and followed Bianca into the clothes shop, while Maeve climbed the winding stairs up to the tower of the Crystal Castle. Afternoon light shone through the tiny, deep-set windows, making warm puddles of gold on the wooden floors. Maeve wasn't sure what she'd been expecting, but Ceridwen, the fortune-teller, looked more like the sandwich lady in the canteen at St Philomena's than a Welsh witch.

'Welcome, Maeve,' she said, glancing at the note that the attendant had sent up. 'You have a beautiful, mystical name.'

'My mum said I was named after a queen, an Irish queen.'

'But before she was a queen, she was a goddess, Mebd. Sometimes they talk about her as Queen Mab of the fairies. In ancient myth, the gods and rulers and ordinary mortals, their stories all intertwine.'

Maeve nodded politely and held out her aura photo. 'The lady who took the photo, she said you could explain what this means. Why am I all red when my friends are all different colours?'

Ceridwen took the photo and frowned as she studied it. 'I'm glad you brought this. It will help enrich your palm-reading. All the arts of divination complement each other. This photo shows you are full of fire, Maeve, the fire of creativity. Red is the colour of the creative life force. But see, there's a little arc of indigo coming into the picture on the left. That's the future. You are going to uncover a deep truth. And then here, this blaze of white, this is your spirit guide. There is someone watching over you. Someone very close to you that has passed over into the spirit world. Perhaps your grandmother, or an older woman close to you.'

Maeve wanted to say it must be her mother but it felt like giving something away. She leant in closer and studied the strange photo, wishing the blaze of white had a face. 'My grandmother is still alive,' she said.

The fortune-teller nodded and took her hand, examining her fingers and stretching them out to their full length.

'The lines on your hand form a pattern, a story woven of all these threads. Look at your life line.' Ceridwen traced the line that ran in an arc between Maeve's thumb and forefinger. 'See how deep it is? That's a sign of your good health and your passion for living. And your head line, here, shows you are a girl of action. Very direct. You act upon your thoughts.'

Maeve thought she spent more time *not* acting upon her thoughts, but she didn't want to contradict the fortune-teller.

As Ceridwen traced the lines on her hand, explaining each one, Maeve tried to picture her mother's hands. Had there been something on her life line that showed she was going to die in a car accident? She could see the way the little finger on Sue's left hand had a kink in it. She could see the perfect half-moons of her cuticles. But she couldn't see the palms. She shut her eyes tight and tried to envision them, but in the end the picture vanished and all she was left with was the whiteness of her mother's hospital bed.

'But what is the spirit guide trying to tell me? What does my palm say I'm meant to do?'

Ceridwen smiled. 'No one can tell you what you have to do. You have to listen to your own inner wisdom, make your own decisions about what's best for you.'

'My grandmother wouldn't want to hear you say that. Or my grandfather. They want to make all the decisions for me.'

'They want to make the right choices for you, but only you can guide them, Maeve. If you're sure of your path, your grandparents will respect your decisions.'

Maeve wanted to say, 'Ha, what do you know?' But she folded her hands in her lap and got up from the table.

'Thank you,' she said. As she walked down the winding staircase she crumpled the aura photo in her hand.

17

In morning light

Maeve woke at dawn. A thin mist lay across the valley and a tiny glimmer of sea sparkled beyond the green hills. She opened the doors of the bungalow and stepped out into the garden. The magnolia tree spread its giant arms above her and the scent was clean and sweet in the morning air. Maeve walked out to the orange grove and took one of the big, mangled uglis from a dark-leafed tree, peeling the thick rind, taking a segment at a time and slipping it in her mouth.

'Boo!' shouted Bianca and Steph, jumping out from behind the fruit trees in their skimpy summer pyjamas.

Maeve lost her balance and fell back into the long, wet grass. 'Now I'm soaking,' she said, laughing as Steph and Bianca hauled her to her feet.

'That's okay,' said Steph. 'We're going swimming.'

Bianca led the way down a narrow track lined with tall, spindly gums that finally opened out beside the dam. A thick mass of pink and gold water lilies clustered at one end and the water sparkled in the morning sunlight.

Bianca immediately stripped off her pyjamas and dived in.

'What if someone comes along?' asked Steph, glancing back along the path.

'Like who? There's no one for miles. And Mum always spends a couple of hours meditating before breakfast. C'mon. Don't be prunes.'

'I think she means prudes,' said Maeve. She didn't need any more encouragement. She peeled off her T-shirt and shorts and followed Bianca into the dam. The water felt warm and silky against her skin, even though the air was cool. She turned onto her back and lay floating, staring up at the pale blue morning sky. Steph finally joined them, though she kept her pyjamas on, just in case.

'I wish we could stay here for ever,' said Maeve.

'Serena says this was a special spirit place for the Arakwal people, you know, the Aborigines from around here,' said Steph. 'I think she said they were called the Bundjalung nation.'

'It must annoy them that a bunch of hippies has taken over,' said Bianca, splashing water at Steph with the flat of her hand.

'Can't you be serious about anything for five minutes?' complained Steph.

'Probably not,' said Bianca. 'You know how shallow I am.'

They started splashing each other wildly, sending plumes of water into the air and making the lilies sway on the rippling surface. Dazzling sun cut through the morning shadows and made every colour sharp, every drop of water shimmer.

Suddenly Maeve felt tired. Something heavy in her chest stopped her from keeping on with the game. She swam to the edge of the dam and climbed out. After putting on her damp pyjamas, she sat on a flat stone, her knees drawn up against her chest.

Steph and Bianca swam towards her.

'What's the matter?' asked Steph, wading out.

'I don't want to go back to Surfers. I want to go to Sydney with you guys. I don't feel like I'm really myself when I'm with my grandparents. It's like they want to wrap me up in cotton wool and I can't breathe. I know they love me but they have this whole scene that I can't be part of. Por Por says I have to make a new life with them, but I liked my old one with you two.'

Steph and Bianca looked at each other, as if they had a secret dialogue that Maeve couldn't be part of. It made her feel even more alone. She picked up a twig and made patterns in the mud around her feet.

'We miss you too,' said Bianca, pulling on her muddied pyjamas. She nudged Maeve to one side and sat down close to her, sharing the rock. 'You'll just have to come back.'

'Like how?' asked Maeve.

'You can be a boarder,' said Bianca. 'Plenty of St Phil's girls are boarders. And then you can spend the weekends with me one week and Steph the next. That way we both get a piece of you. I can't believe you wanted to go and live at Steph's house instead of mine.'

Steph put her arm around Maeve's shoulder and hugged her. 'See, we've figured it all out.'

'Why didn't you say so before?'

'We weren't sure you wanted to come back. I mean you have that cool room to yourself and the beach outside and we didn't know if you wanted to leave.'

Maeve jabbed her drawing stick into the muddy ground. 'But how do I tell my grandparents? I don't want to hurt them.'

'Love hurts,' said Bianca, shrugging.

'That's not very helpful,' said Steph reproachfully. 'Maeve, what would your mum have wanted you to do?'

Maeve stared out over the water at the thick forest beyond. 'I think she would have wanted me to be near Ned. She didn't have any brothers or sisters, so that was important to her.'

'Brothers are such a waste of time,' said Bianca. 'I am so glad I'm an only child.'

'Will you shut up!' said Steph, scooping up a handful of mud and flinging it at Bianca. Bianca squealed and made a dive at her.

Before Maeve could stop them, they were rolling around on the muddy bank of the dam. How could she make any important decisions with these two crazy people as her advisors? She scraped her fingers through the thick gooey sludge and gathered up two handfuls of ammunition.

'If you can't beat 'em, join 'em!' she shouted, diving into the fray.

18

The Book of Changes

Maeve took a deep breath as she walked through the entrance to Azalea Apartments. It had been hard watching Steph and Bianca pass through the gates at Coolangatta airport without her. But the conversation she was about to have with her grandparents was going to be much harder.

Por Por and Goong Goong were sitting on the balcony drinking tea and reading the morning papers when Maeve let herself into the apartment. She put her bag in her room and went to join them, her stomach full of butterflies as she rehearsed in her mind what she was about to say. There was no point waiting for the right moment. If she didn't say what she was thinking now, she might never have the courage. She sat between them and reached over to put her hand on her grandmother's.

'Goong Goong, Por Por, I can't go to Ingleside College. I did a lot of thinking when I was in Byron. I have to go back to Sydney. I want to go back to St Philomena's as a boarder.'

Goong Goong's face didn't show a flicker of emotion but Por Por almost dropped her teacup.

'But Ingleside is a good school! A good school where you will make good new friends.'

'St Philomena's was a good school and I already have good old friends, Por Por. I have to go back to Sydney. I miss my friends and I miss Ned. Mum would have wanted me to be there for him. I have to go back.'

Por Por pulled her hand away. Talking about Ned was painful for Por Por. She had wanted Ned to come to Queensland too.

'Heaps of girls live in the boarding school at St Phil's,' said Maeve, talking quickly, not wanting to give Por Por an opportunity to think up too many arguments. 'And I can come up to Surfers in all the holidays. And we can see each other for weekends in Sydney when you're at Potts Point. St Philomena's has a really top music and drama department and that's important to me.'

Por Por took off her tortoise-shell reading glasses and put them down on the table with such force that Maeve thought they might break.

'Music and drama!' she said. 'What about science and maths! What about your Chinese!' She looked to Goong Goong, trying to encourage him to back her up, but he returned her gaze impassively.

Maeve turned to her grandfather, appealing to him with both hands folded as if in prayer.

'I'll learn Chinese too,' she said. 'I will work so hard. You won't be sorry. I promise.'

Goong Goong turned away, as if he couldn't bear to look at her earnest face full of longing.

'This is not a decision for you to make,' he said. Then he turned to Por Por and began to speak to her in Chinese, his voice low but each sentence finishing with an emphatic sharpness. Maeve pushed her chair away from the table in disgust and went straight to her room, slamming the door behind her.

Maeve's brain felt fuzzy with rage. When she logged on to MSN, there were six people on line. Before she even had time to write anything, Dancing Man sent her a message. *Where U been WPKA?*

Slumming in Byron, answered Maeve.

Cool.

I hate 13.

?

I wanna be 18. Be the boss of my own life.

14 is cool. I dig 14. Sexy body, good times, no responsibilities. Jk. lol.

lol. Gtg.

Maeve logged off in disgust. How had this guy got into her address book? She blocked him and opened her email to write a long, frustrated rant to Steph and Bianca. She was so engrossed in writing that it was only when Por Por sat down on the edge of her bed that she realised she was no longer alone.

'Siu Siu, when I was a little girl like you and I had to make a serious decision, my grandmother would consult the *I Ching*. The Book of Changes is what some people call it. Perhaps now is a good time for me to teach you how to use this. I don't want to fight with you. The *I Ching* will help both of us find answers.'

'Do you believe in that sort of thing?' asked Maeve.

'I believe that the world is always torn between order and chaos. And that the *I Ching* can help you find a way forward.' Por Por got up from the bed and stretched her hand out to Maeve. 'I will teach you as my grandmother taught me,' she said.

In the living room, Por Por went to the lacquered enamel cabinet and took out a long bamboo tube and a weathered old brown book.

She ran her hand along the tablecloth, smoothing out every wrinkle, and sat down with Maeve opposite her. 'Now first, you must make a question and hold that question in your mind,' said Por Por.

'Like, should I go to boarding school?' asked Maeve, half expecting Por Por to complain about the question.

'That's right,' said Por Por. 'Now you hold the question and you take the yarrow sticks that you find in this container and build a *gua*, a hexagram that we can interpret to find the answer to your question.'

Following Por Por's instructions, Maeve laid out the skinny yarrow sticks, counting them into groups of four and then picking up the remaining twigs and continuing to lay them out in more groups of four. It felt confusing at first, but slowly the task became rhythmic. Each time Maeve laid them out, Por Por made a note of what number Maeve's pattern symbolised. When she'd repeated the task five more times, Por Por opened the Book of Changes.

Maeve leapt up and tried to read over her grandmother's shoulder. The pages of the book were of thick, yellowing paper and all the writing was in complex Chinese characters.

'The fifty-sixth *gua*,' said Por Por, sighing. '*Lu*, a quest, a journey, you will stay in places other than your home, a lodger, surrounded by others that are also on a quest.

A stranger in a strange land . . .' Her voice was heavy.

'I don't get it. Does that mean staying here, or does that mean going to boarding school?'

Suddenly, Goong Goong was standing at the end of the dining-room table, gazing down at the *gua*. 'It means that you should go to boarding school,' he said firmly.

19

A single creased envelope

Maeve pulled her doona over her head. She wished Vivienne would stop talking. It was after midnight.

Vivienne was so homesick that she phoned her friends and family in Malaysia every night on her mobile. She was trying to speak quietly but every now and then she'd give a little squeal of laughter and it would drag Maeve back from the edge of sleep. She could dob her in, go and complain about her at the office in the morning, but that would be plain mean. Boarders had to stick together.

Maeve rolled over and tapped the wall beside her bed three times, listening for the response. When the seven short taps came in reply, she slipped out of bed, picked up her Maglite and padded down the corridor.

Gina was reading by torchlight when Maeve tiptoed into her dorm. 'Is blabbermouth at it again?' she whispered.

Maeve nodded and sat down on the end of Gina's bed. 'I wish they'd put me in here with you,' she grumbled.

Gina laughed softly. 'I'd drive you crazy too, girl,' she said.

'I've never had to share a room with anyone before.

Except my baby brother, and he didn't really count. He just made cute little snuffly noises.'

'Lucky you don't come from my family,' said Gina. 'I shared with three sisters but they were a lot noisier than this mob.' She gestured towards the three sleeping figures in the other beds.

Gina pushed her ear against the wall. 'I reckon Viv is going to be talking all night.' She lifted up the doona and wriggled over to make room for Maeve. 'I've got to get up early for training, so you'd better not kick me in your sleep.'

Maeve giggled and got in beside her. 'Talk about kicking. You kick like a bloody kangaroo. Everyone reckons you're gonna be the next Cathy Freeman.'

'McCabe thinks that's pretty funny. You know he got me a music scholarship to come here?'

'I thought you got a sports scholarship.'

'Yeah, everyone thinks that, but you know that Koori singer, Rosie Malloy?'

'Nope,' said Maeve, yawning sleepily.

'You're a city slicker, that's why. She sings country, like Kasey Chambers except she's really old, like a legend. She came to Tamworth and heard me sing and dobbed me in to McCabe. Next thing I know, I'm on a train down here. Then they find out I can run too, and so next year I'm gonna have a sports scholarship and McCabe's going to give the music scholarship to someone else. That bloke is a serious do-gooder.'

'Don't you like being here?'

'Sure, it's good. But it's not like being at home, is it?'

Maeve snuggled down under the bedding and tried to make enough space for herself on the edge of the mattress. She hadn't imagined that life in the boarding school would be like this – so crowded, so full of gossip and new people. And so not like a home. When she'd read the Harry Potter books she'd imagined that boarding school might be like a home away from home, but it was more like a secret club. During the day, the boarders avoided each other. It was as if your life depended on having other friends that kept you connected to the real world. Nothing belonged to you, nothing was permanent, everyone had lives somewhere else that were more important than anything that happened in the boarding house. It was nothing like Hogwarts.

Maeve woke up to find Gina gone and the rest of the dormitory scrambling to get organised for the school day. She trudged back to her room and looked at the mess of papers and homework that covered her desk. She was glad it was Friday.

The best thing about Fridays was Ned. After school, Maeve caught the bus over to Balmain and ran all the way back to her old home. Somehow, when she was with Ned, everything seemed to make sense. He was growing up fast, starting to look more like a little boy and less like a toddler. But when he wrapped his arms tight around her neck and pressed his face into her shoulder, Maeve could almost imagine that they still lived together under the same roof, that nothing had changed for them.

On that hot Friday afternoon, Maeve filled the paddle pool and dressed Ned in his bathers. A magpie laughed as Ned squealed and splashed in the shade of the gum tree. At first Maeve sat and watched, but the heat was so intense that she soon peeled off her socks and sandals and jumped in beside him. She didn't even bother to take off her school uniform.

'Whoops,' said Ned, laughing as he filled a plastic cup with water and tipped it on Maeve's head. They were still splashing in the pool when Andy came home from the supermarket. He called down to them from the kitchen window and Ned waved back, shouting 'Dad! Dad! Dad!'

Maeve hauled Ned out of the water and carried him up the back steps. They sat dripping on the doorstep, eating icypoles while Andy put away the shopping.

'Maybe you should nip upstairs and get something dry to wear over to Steph's,' said Andy.

'I'm not going to Steph's tonight. She has to work, and Bianca has a date. We're meeting up tomorrow morning instead. I don't mind going back to school all wet,' said Maeve.

'You could take something of Sue's. I've been meaning to ask you to take what you want. I'll have to do something with her clothes when we move.'

'You're not going to move, really?' asked Maeve, turning to stare at Andy in dismay.

'I can't hold out against your grandparents, Maeve. Besides, the place is too big with just me and Ned rattling around in it. We don't use the extra rooms and I need a new start. I was thinking maybe we'll move up to Byron. It's closer to my parents so they can help me out with Ned more.'

'But that's miles away from me! I'll never get to see Ned if you take him away from Sydney. And this is our home. I mean, what if I want to come back and live here?'

'Live with me?' asked Andy, incredulous. 'You know your grandparents would have a fit. Jesus, they'd take Ned off me if they could.'

'But what if I want to come back, when I'm eighteen? They couldn't stop me then!'

'Honey, I'm not your father.'

Maeve felt her face blushing crimson and she pressed her hands against her cheeks. She dropped the icypole on the steps, leapt to her feet and ran through the kitchen, taking the stairs up to the second floor two at a time.

She'd run to her bedroom on instinct. As soon as she opened the door and looked in at the piles of boxes and stripped-down bed, a wave of misery washed over her. She slammed the door and ran back along the hallway, straight to the main bedroom, a long, elegant room with doors opening on to the upstairs balcony. As soon as she'd shut the door, she regretted coming in here too.

When Maeve was little, she used to climb into her mother's big bed and press her face against the pillows. There was something sweet and warm and comforting about the smell that used to make her feel calmer. But it didn't smell like her mother's room any more. It had a stale, sweaty man's smell, and Andy's clothes lay in piles on every piece of furniture.

Maeve slid open the doors of the wardrobe. She ran her hand across the clothes, feeling the softness of her mother's silk blouses, the coarse texture of the winter coat. She buried her face in them. It was terrible to think that anyone but Sue should wear these clothes. Tears coursed down her cheeks as she stripped them from their hangers and threw them in a pile on the floor. Each item of clothing stirred a memory of an event, a moment Maeve had shared with her mother, that made her chest ache.

Maeve knelt on the floor and took out each pair of shoes, cradling them in her hands. They were so tiny! She crawled into the back of the cupboard and pulled out all the old shoeboxes, folding back the tissue paper to uncover the history of her mother's shoes. The very last box felt lighter than the others. When Maeve lifted the lid she discovered it held a pile of letters. Most of the letters were in Por Por's handwriting. Maeve didn't want to read those. It felt too much like prying into Por Por's business. There was also a small collection of pale blue envelopes from Andy. Then, right at the bottom of the shoebox, there was a single creased envelope with unfamiliar handwriting on the front. It was covered in stamps from Nepal and Maeve knew, instantly, that it had to be the letter her mother had told her about, the letter from her father. Inside were folds of fine onionskin paper covered with small drawings and words.

As she separated the sheets, a strip of passport photos fell to the floor. The face that looked up at her was sharp and craggy. Maeve cupped the photos in her hand and studied her father's features. His eyes were so pale, they looked as if they could be colourless. His dark hair was matted in thick curly dreadlocks, and he stared at the camera with an intensity that made her shiver. She thought of Andy's friendly face. But she couldn't compare them. Andy wasn't her father. He'd said so himself.

Maeve took a long purple shawl from the pile of clothes behind her and wrapped it around the letter. Swiftly she stripped off her uniform and slipped into a free-fitting cotton dress. It had reached the ground when her mother wore it, but it only came halfway up Maeve's calves. Without allowing herself to cry, she picked out a couple of shirts, a jumper and a single pair of winter gloves from the pile of discarded clothing. She gathered up her wet uniform and padded back downstairs, the letter from her father tightly bound in the web of her mother's clothes.

20

A promise to break

Maeve stuck the photo of her father in the green notebook and stuffed the book into her dance bag. She couldn't wait to show Bianca and Steph. But when she arrived for dance class next morning, they weren't there. After she had worked through the first routine and neither of her friends had arrived, she checked her mobile, but there were no messages. Finally, when they were finishing the tap class, Maeve asked Louise if she knew where they were.

'Oh, didn't Steph tell you? They've given her a permanent Saturday shift at Macca's down in Darling Harbour. She's won't be able to make it at all on Saturdays from now on.'

Maeve felt a cold knot form in her stomach. 'And Bianca?'

'That little vixen! I have no idea. Do you know where she was on Tuesday night? This is the third class she's missed. I'm going to have to have a word to her parents.'

Maeve backed away, not wanting to make trouble for Bianca. Somehow, she couldn't lose herself in the dance for the rest of the morning. Nothing came easily.

She was struggling through the theme to *Fame* when

McCabe came into the hall. Maeve was a little surprised to see him there but more intriguing was his companion, a tall, spiky-haired younger man. They each took a seat on stage and watched the class progress. The spiky-haired man scribbled something into his notebook and showed it to McCabe, who nodded.

When the classes drew to a close, McCabe and his companion took Louise to one side and the three stood in a huddle talking. Maeve slumped out into Darling Street and sat alone, waiting for her bus.

She pulled out the green notebook and turned to the page with her father's photograph. He definitely looked scary. Maeve tried to see how she and he looked alike. Sue's face had been round but Maeve's was longer and narrower like her father's. The shape of his mouth, the long, thin lips and the dimple in his left cheek hinted at a smile that was like Maeve's, but there was also something dark and disturbing in his face that she didn't want to dwell on. It made her glad that Steph and Bianca hadn't been there to see the picture. She turned the page and began to write.

*I used to be the one that everyone could talk to.
People would tell me things. But since the accident,
everyone is scared. Because something so bad happened
to me, maybe they think I'm jinxed. Even B & S forget
to tell me things, as if they're afraid for me and of me.*

Her mobile beeped. *Urgent. Meet us @ Rozelle Mkts. Waiting for u. S*

When Maeve got off the bus, Steph rushed up and hugged her, as if she'd been waiting.

'Total emergency. Omar has dumped Bunka,' said Steph, her face furrowed with concern.

'What?' said Maeve. 'When? Why didn't she call me?'

'Ask her. She brought him to Macca's this morning and they had a fight, right there, while I was on my shift! He stormed out and Bunka sat there crying until I knocked off. I'm so glad you're here. I thought some retail therapy might cheer her up, but she won't even buy anything.'

The markets were held in the grounds of the old primary school. Steph and Maeve wove their way through the crowds to where Bianca was standing in a doorway with '1887' carved in the stone lintel above. Only a few metres from where she stood, other girls were flipping through racks of brightly coloured clothes, holding up strands of shiny beads that glittered in the afternoon sunlight, but Bianca didn't seem to notice any of it.

'Why didn't you call me?' said Maeve, hugging her tightly.

'You would have been at dance class. I didn't want the whole world to know I'd been dumped. Bastard. I hate him.'

Maeve looked to Steph and raised her eyebrows. 'Why don't we all go and get something to eat. Pide?'

It was a ritual that they each bought a cheese and spinach pide for lunch and sat on the stone footings of the old school fence beneath the Marketman sign, a picture of an alternative Superman who advertised the Saturday market.

Bianca picked at her pide, nibbling at the spinach and flicking bits of cheese onto the footpath.

'I was going to dump him, but he got in first. That's what happened. That has to be what happened. I wasn't fast enough.'

'What did he say?' asked Maeve.

'Get this, he said his parents didn't approve of me. Me! Like I wasn't doing him the favour going out with him in the first place. They think I'm a Skip and that Skips have no values and that he was too young to have a girlfriend and he should stick with football. How insulting is that!'

'They probably would have been cool if you were Lebanese,' said Steph.

Maeve wasn't so sure. 'That's just parents being freaked out about the whole girlfriend issue. It's not about you, Bunka.'

'But I'm not a Skip,' said Bianca, starting to cry. 'My grandfather was Italian. That means I'm Italian, doesn't it?'

Maeve and Steph looked at each other and then both hooked an arm through Bianca's and dragged her to her feet. Maeve took Bianca's pide away from her and threw it in the bin.

'Time for emergency cheering-up treatment,' she said.

They crossed the busy street, dodging the traffic, and led Bianca into the cool interior of Café 2000. As if to prove she really was Italian, Bianca ordered her gelati in Italian and when the waiter answered her with something flirtatious, she laughed. Maeve and Steph smiled at each other, relieved.

When they were settled behind one of the little blue tables, Maeve realised Steph didn't have a gelati.

'I'm saving up for the drama trip,' said Steph. 'I'll just have a taste of yours.'

'But they don't let any Year 9 students go on that trip,' said Maeve. 'You haven't got a hope.'

'Not this year, next year. As if I could save enough money between now and April! I don't think so! It took Jess Turner nearly two years to earn her fare. But you get to tour London and Ireland. I so want to go! If I start saving now, then I should have enough money by Year 10, and Mum and Dad said if I could cover my expenses then they'd chip in for the airfare.'

'Ireland,' said Maeve. 'It would be incredible.'

'I'd rather go to Italy,' said Bianca. 'Italy is way cooler. I loved Venice so much. London is okay but it's kind of grungy.'

Steph and Maeve didn't say anything. It was one of those annoying things about Bianca. Her parents had already taken her around the world twice. She'd been to Disneyland on three continents. It was hard to talk about going anywhere in front of her.

'Well, it is a drama trip anyway,' said Steph. 'You're more a dance and music person. It's for people interested in theatre and history. It's not a tourist trip – like, it's serious. They do drama workshops in London and Dublin.'

Dublin. Maeve shivered at the prospect. What if she was allowed on the tour? The idea sent her mind racing. Did her father go back to Ireland? And if he did, where was he? She could see why her mother had never shown her the letter or the photo. Somehow, having that single paper clue made it even more maddening that he couldn't be found.

'My grandparents would never let me go,' she said.

'I might go,' said Bianca. 'If I can talk the 'rents around. I could tell them that it would help heal my broken heart.'

'But it's not until next year. You won't still be broken-hearted in a year's time.'

'I might be,' said Bianca, stabbing a poco roll into her gelati. 'Or I might make Omar really suffer by getting a new boyfriend right now. Then I could dump him before next year's tour.'

'Like who?' asked Maeve. 'Josh?'

'No, Josh is up himself. 'Dancing Man' – you know, the one who sends the cute messages.'

'Have you even met him?' asked Maeve.

'Yeah,' said Bianca, her shoulders slumping. 'But it wouldn't make Omar jealous. Problem is, Dancing Man's a short-arse. I think you saw him that time we were shopping in Newtown. He goes to the performing arts school. He'll be auditioning for that show that McCabe has been trying to get everyone involved in.'

'What show?' asked Maeve.

'It's some big joint production called *Seussmania* being staged by a bunch of community theatre troupes around Strathfield. They're looking for heaps of kids to be extras.'

'McCabe was at dance this morning with some dude but he didn't say anything. And why didn't you guys tell me about it? Nobody tells me anything any more.'

Bianca and Steph looked at each other and shrugged.

'You're always doing stuff after school now,' said Steph. 'You seem really busy and you always say you have to call us back when we try and organise anything.'

'That's not my fault. That's my grandparents. I have to get permission to do anything outside school. Sometimes I feel like I have to get permission to sneeze.'

'Are they scared you're going to run away again?'

'I didn't really run away. I mean, where would I run to?'

'Let's all run away to Ireland next year,' said Steph. 'The Three Musketeers take on the world!'

'I thought you said the drama tour was too serious for an airhead like me,' said Bianca.

'I did not!' said Steph. 'You're just looking for an excuse to feel sorry for yourself. Face it. Omar's a dickhead. You're gorgeous and you know it! Do you want to go on the drama tour or not?'

'Of course. You two can't go without me!'

'So it's agreed,' said Steph, putting her hand out so they could forge their pact. 'All for one and Ireland for all.'

Maeve's hand lay firm and steady between Bianca's and Steph's, but secretly she felt worried. Was she making a promise her grandparents would never let her keep?

21

Seussmania

Maeve wished Steph had come to the audition as well. Bianca was making her nervous. She was so edgy, so keen to get a role in the show. Maeve wanted one too. She'd seen the older performers in rehearsal – they came from performing arts schools all over Sydney, from Strathmore TAFE, from Newtown. There was even a student from NIDA who was directing the show.

Maeve did some warm-ups, stretching her legs against the wall, making her muscles work until they stung. The pain felt good, distracting her from the fizzing inside her head.

A tall, lanky man with a red-and-white top hat under his arm walked past them, his cat's tail swishing out behind him.

'That's the Cat in the Hat,' squealed Bianca. 'Did you see? That's the Cat! I so want to be Sally. It would be so cool to be Sally.'

'She's probably already cast,' said Maeve. 'McCabe said it's only extras that they're looking for. We might wind up as a teapot and a spoon or something like that. They're making all the furniture into people and throwing in a few spare Grinches.'

'There's no Grinch in *The Cat in the Hat*,' said Bianca.

'I don't think it's the straight story. Some weird mixed-up version of it. Like they've taken all the characters from all Seuss's books and chucked them in together.'

Maeve was glad to see McCabe making his way towards them through the crowd of performers. Beside him was a man in another tall, striped top hat, the same guy who had sat in on her dance class.

'Maeve, Bianca, this is my son Will. Will, these are two of my students from St Phil's.'

'Cool,' said Will. 'I'll look forward to seeing what you can do. I'm director of the show, which I think Dad failed to mention.' Will looked at his watch. 'We're running a little behind. Another twenty minutes, maybe?' Maeve caught a glimpse of a bright tattoo on his wrist of the fish from *The Cat in the Hat*.

'Did you have that done specially for the show?' she asked.

McCabe winced. Will caught his dad's expression and laughed. 'I've been into Seuss for a long time. I've got Thing One and Thing Two tattooed on my shoulders, one each side.'

McCabe groaned and shook his head in mock disbelief. It was hard to believe they were father and son. The two men moved on and Bianca nudged Maeve in the ribs. Maeve knew exactly what she was thinking.

'He's too old for you,' she whispered.

'I can dream, can't I?'

'I didn't know McCabe was married. He told me he used to be a priest and then he was a musician. Or it might have been the other way around.'

'Maybe Will is why he had to stop being a priest,' said Bianca. 'Maybe he found out that Will was his long-lost son from some affair or something.'

Maeve looked at Will and McCabe as they sat in the middle of the stalls of the darkened theatre. Maybe that's what McCabe had meant about secret lives. She wondered if her dad had guessed that she was alive. Perhaps he knew that she was out here, waiting for him. Perhaps he'd find her one day, as McCabe had found Will. Or maybe she'd have to go looking for him.

Bianca and Maeve were herded into a backstage area to wait their turn. The air was pungent with the odour of dust and sweat. A hushed excitement fell as the teenagers were sorted into groups and marched out on stage. A young woman with thick dark hair tied up in a topknot showed them the routine she wanted them to perform and they followed her through the movements.

'Turn, three, four, step, turn, one, two . . .' The instructions moved from Maeve's mind into her body and she flowed through the routine effortlessly. When she turned around, she was surprised to see Bianca pulling a face, her forehead beaded with sweat.

The lines of dancers were rearranged and when Maeve was behind Bianca she realised what the problem was. Bianca was slightly out of sync with the other dancers. To make matters worse, there was a boy dancing beside her who moved so smoothly that Bianca looked even less on top of the routine. Maeve found herself staring at the boy's back, wishing he'd make a mistake so that Bianca would look better.

When he turned around, Maeve had a weird sensation of

having met him before. He stared at her with piercing green eyes and then, self-consciously, tried to pat down a cowlick of dark hair that stood up on one side of his head.

'Hey,' he said, smiling a lopsided smile that made his whole face light up.

'Hey,' replied Maeve. She could feel a warm blush moving from her chest to her face and she turned away quickly.

Will came on stage and started talking to the dance instructor while they all stood around, stretching, waiting for the next set of instructions. Bianca sidled over to Maeve. 'I so messed that up,' she grumbled. 'It was that kid next to me. He really put me off my stride.'

'He's so annoying,' said Maeve. 'I know I've seen him somewhere before but I can't figure where.'

'He's Jackson. That kid I was telling you about from Newtown. He's all yours if you want him. Definitely too young for me.'

'You're kidding?' said Maeve. 'He's Dancing Man?'

Bianca nodded but before Maeve could find out more, the boy crossed the stage to where they stood.

'Will wants you and me to do the routine together. Just the two of us.'

'Who? Me?' said Maeve, looking over her shoulder.

'Yeah, you,' said the boy. 'You're Maeve, aren't you? I'm Jackson,' he said, tipping his head on one side, as if he were doing some sort of secret calculation. 'You're Warrior Princess, aren't you? Let's see if you really can kick arse.'

The other dancers sat or stood around the edge of the stage. Maeve looked at Jackson for a split second before turning all her attention to Will and the dance instructor.

'I hear you're a bit of a gymnast,' said Will.

'Not any more,' said Maeve, alarmed. 'My mum made me stop. She thought it was bad for my body.'

'But you can still remember some of the moves? I can tell, watching you, that some of that gymnastics training is still with you. Your kinaesthetic memory looks to be pretty sharp.'

'Kines-what?' asked Maeve.

'Kinaesthetic memory – it's the way we recall movement. Some people talk about it as kinaesthetic intelligence. Kinaesthesia is the way your body, your muscles, sense movement and weight and position.'

'I guess I'm okay at that. I can still do a few things. Like handsprings and backward walkovers.'

'Okay, great,' said Will. 'I want you two to work through the same routine as before, but I want you to finish with a handspring and then into splits. Is that asking too much?'

'No, easy-peasey,' said Maeve, looking at Jackson. 'Is that okay with you?'

'Don't worry about Jackson,' said Will, cuffing the boy over the head. 'He can turn himself into a pretzel if he wants.'

The music started and Maeve fell into the routine as if it was one she'd performed every day of her life. When the dance instructor called 'Now!', she and Jackson threw themselves forward and bounced into handsprings, then slid smoothly into the splits. Maeve had never seen a boy who could do the splits with such ease. At dance class, all the guys winced as they eased themselves down to the floor but Jackson acted as if his muscles and joints were made of rubber.

Later, as they milled around in the backstage area along with the rest of the cast, Jackson came up and stood with Bianca. 'You were good, you know, Bianca, even if your timing was a little out.'

'She knows she's good,' said Maeve. Bianca and Jackson both looked at her, surprised at the ferocity in her voice. Even Maeve was surprised at herself. Sometimes when she stood next to Bianca she felt completely invisible, but usually she didn't care. Why did she want Jackson to notice her anyway?

'Well, thanks,' said Bianca. 'You were amazing. I mean, you so are going to have a serious part. You and Maeve. God, I'll be glad if they let me be a teapot. I know I stuffed up majorly.'

Maeve had never felt jealous of Bianca before but suddenly she wanted to be the one talking to Jackson. Why did she feel so tongue-tied? Why did it annoy her that Jackson was smiling at Bianca? What did it matter?

'Will is my sort-of cousin so it's kind of nepotistic. I mean, he knows what I can do and that I'd be totally pissed if he didn't give me a good part.'

'Are you related to McCabe too?' asked Bianca.

'Sort of. He's kind of my uncle.'

'What do you mean "kind of"?'

'Well, my granny adopted him when he was a teenager. My mum is his little sister. He's like my godfather. It's kind of complicated but he's a cool guy, even if he is a teacher.'

The lists went up on the board as they talked and a crowd of teenagers surged forward to see who'd been cast.

'I told you I'd be a teapot,' said Bianca gloomily as she

stood on her tiptoes reading the names over the heads of the others. Maeve elbowed her way forward, until she was right in front of the list.

'You're not a teapot – you're a ... ohhhh ... an umbrella stand,' she said, her voice trailing off. She traced her finger down the list of chorus dancers but couldn't see her own name. 'I didn't get a part,' she said, disbelieving.

Suddenly, Jackson was standing beside her. 'Look up here,' he said, pointing. 'You and me. We're Thing One and Thing Two.'

22

WPKA

Maeve had never spent so much time with a boy before, except for Ned. And that definitely didn't count. Working with Jackson made her feel like a different person. Two evenings a week and nearly all day Sunday, she and Jackson twirled and bounced their way across the stage during the rehearsals of *Seussmania*. As the opening night of the show drew closer, Maeve began to feel as though she and Jackson really were Thing One and Thing Two, two crazy creatures that could conjure mischief and mayhem with a flick of their wrists. Jackson was always in motion. Maeve couldn't imagine him being still for more than five seconds. Even when he was standing around waiting for his call, Jackson would be doing something with his hands. Whether he was juggling, doing card tricks or practising a weird version of Tai Chi in front of a mirror, Jackson was always in motion.

'You are so vain,' said Maeve teasingly. 'I reckon you just do that Tai Chi so you can have an excuse to stare at yourself.'

Jackson laughed. 'It's not Tai Chi, dummy. It's a martial art called Wing Chun. I'm practising my form.'

'So you bore people to death by forcing them to watch you make all those little gestures.'

'It's a type of kung fu. Will does it too. So should you. You shouldn't count on me being around to protect you forever.'

'Funny ha ha,' said Maeve, drawing herself up to her full height and trying to look down on Jackson. Tactfully, he ignored her.

As they stood side by side, she studied their reflections in the mirror. They were both dressed in bright red costumes like baby jumpsuits, and blue wigs. They looked so much like little kids, it made Maeve want to laugh.

'I'm actually three centimetres taller than you, you know,' she said. Jackson stopped practising and turned to look at her.

'No way. Bianca!' he called. 'Grab a book or something. This chick reckons she's taller than me.'

They took off their wigs and turned back to back, their heels touching, their backs flush against each other. Maeve could feel the sharpness of Jackson's bones, the warmth of his body against her own.

Bianca laid the spine of her maths book across the top of their heads. 'Sorry, Jackson,' she said. 'Maeve is definitely taller than you.'

'Crap,' said Jackson, turning around and standing on tiptoes, stretching so his chin was higher than Maeve's. 'Just give me time. One day, Maeve Kwong, you are going to get a crick in your neck looking up at me.'

Maeve laughed. 'Maybe I'd better come along to that martial arts class before you catch up with me.'

When Maeve phoned Por Por to ask permission to attend the martial arts class, Por Por wasn't impressed.

'But it's a *Chinese* martial art,' said Maeve.

'Between dance classes and this play, you never sit still! When will you have time to study?'

The summer with her grandparents had been like living in a cocoon and Maeve was desperate to spread her wings. But she couldn't tell Por Por that's how she felt, nor could she tell her about Jackson. There were so many small secrets that she had to keep from her grandmother. It took another ten minutes of pleading, but eventually she talked Por Por around.

The house mother wasn't happy either. She gave Maeve a long lecture about the number of outside school activities she was already involved with. Maeve hung her head and let the words wash over her, but she didn't give up. She hated spending her evenings in the common room, arguing with Gina and Viv about whose turn it was to use the remote. Eventually, McCabe smoothed the way, finalising the permission slips and even arranging for Will and his girlfriend to pick her up from school.

On Wednesday night, Maeve stood waiting in the school foyer for Will to arrive. A stream of parents filed into the multi-purpose room. Maeve stood by the open door and watched as Ms Donahue screened a video of last year's drama club trip. Senior girls stood with their arms linked in front of ancient stone cottages, hiked across deep green fields and posed in front of theatre posters. The tour ran for nearly three weeks, with half that time spent in

England and the other half in Ireland.

A Powerpoint presentation showed highlights of Dublin: famous streets, green parks and crowds of people standing outside the Abbey Theatre. Maeve found herself wondering if one of those faces in the crowd could be her father. Maybe he was captured for a split second in one of those frames. She leant forward, frowning. He probably wasn't there. He was probably still somewhere in Nepal, completely out of reach.

Maeve tried not to stare at Will as she sat in the back of his beaten-up old station wagon. In profile, he looked a lot like his father. But there were things about him that were nothing like McCabe. Maeve couldn't stop thinking about Bianca's suggestion that Will was a long-lost son. If it was true, then how had he and his father found each other? She wriggled uncomfortably in her seat, trying to think of a way to ask him. Will's girlfriend, Lauren, politely tried to include Maeve in their conversation but there was only one thing Maeve wanted to talk about. Finally she blurted out a question that she hoped would lead somewhere.

'Is your mum going to come to the show when it opens?' she asked.

Lauren fell silent and Maeve knew she'd said something wrong. Will glanced over his shoulder quickly and then turned back to concentrate on the road. 'My mum died of cancer when I was sixteen, but my brothers will probably turn up. And of course, Dad will be there. I don't think he's missed a single show I've ever been part of, from the kindergarten nativity play upwards.'

Maeve squirmed with embarrassment.

'Sorry about your mum,' she said.

'Hey, it's okay. I know you lost your mother too. That first year is tough. Everything changes so fast. Just hang in there, Maeve.'

'I'm trying,' she said. 'But sorry, I know this is weird, and none of my business . . . but I thought your dad said he'd been a priest.'

'He was for a while. He left the priesthood to marry Mum. It must have been so bad for him when she died and he was on his own with me and my brothers. We all went berserk for a while, but Dad pulled us through.'

Light and shadow flickered across Will's face and for a moment Maeve could see that he was remembering his mother. She knew that feeling, when all the hurt came rushing to the surface and then somehow you managed to push it back down. How could people who'd had bad things happen to them look so normal most of the time? She looked down at her own body, amazed at how much hurt, how many painful things she could keep inside it and never show the world.

The Wing Chun class was held in an old building in Leichhardt, above a coffee shop. As they climbed the stairs to the second floor, the sharp, rich scent of ground coffee made Maeve feel awake and alert. It seemed to have permeated the walls of the building. Two sides of the studio upstairs were lined with mirrors. Rows of men and women in white stood practising a series of hand gestures in front of their reflections.

'I thought this was a martial arts class,' said Maeve. 'Doesn't anyone fight?'

'Wing Chun is different to other martial arts,' said Lauren. 'It's not about brute strength, it's about neutralising your enemy. It's the only martial art that was invented by a woman, so it's very precise.'

Maeve smiled. 'That's cool. But does that mean I won't get to hit Jackson?'

Will laughed. 'They say that Ng Mui, the Shaolin nun who developed it, came up with the idea after watching a rat fight with a crane. That's why Jackson digs it. I've got to concentrate to keep ahead of him!'

Lauren shook her head. 'Will's being modest. He's already a Si-Hing, which means he's a senior student, and soon he'll be a trainee instructor.'

'I don't know,' said Will. 'Jackson's pretty good. He's got a big advantage being fourteen. He'll slaughter me in a couple of years time.'

'I'm fourteen next month,' said Maeve.

'That's a good age. Wing Chun was only fifteen when she became Ng Mui's student,' said Lauren. 'She was really beautiful but was bullied by this guy who tried to force her to marry him. So Ng Mui taught her to fight and then she challenged the bully to a fight and beat the shit out of him. The technique was named after her.'

'That's why Lauren comes along,' joked Will. 'Trying to keep me from bullying her.' Lauren punched him playfully on the shoulder and then went to join her sparring partner.

Will led Maeve to the end of the room and introduced her to the instructor. When the students had finished practising, Maeve was paired with Jackson, who showed her the Wing Chun stance and the basic position for fighting. Then they practised a move where Jackson had to grab her from behind and the instructor showed her how to free herself from his grip.

'So, Warrior Princess,' whispered Jackson, when the instructor had moved on to the next pair of students. 'Time you really learned how to kick arse.'

Maeve could feel the warmth from his body, even though he was centimetres away from her. Her heart started to beat faster as she waited for him to grab her again. As his arm encircled her neck, she caught the salty sweet smell of his skin. Instinctively, she executed the move the instructor had taught her, tracking her heel down Jackson's leg and ramming it into the crown of his foot while elbowing him in the ribs at the same time.

Jackson let out a grunt of pain, lost his balance and fell onto the mats. Maeve put her hand over her mouth, appalled at how hard she'd hit him.

'Sorry!' she said. 'I didn't think it would work that well.'

'I'm all right,' said Jackson, getting to his feet slowly. 'But next time, just try and maim me. You can kill me when the show closes, okay?'

23

Auld lang syne

The excitement backstage was like a shimmering electric energy that made the air itself seem to throw off sparks. Maeve and Jackson sat side by side in front of the mirrors in the dressing room while the make-up girls finished drawing in their high, arched eyebrows. It made them look slightly deranged, with their spiky blue wigs and their faces painted flat white. Jackson touched Maeve's shoulder as they stood together stage left, waiting for their call.

'Break a leg,' he said. 'But not one of mine, okay?'

'What if I stuff up?' said Maeve, stepping from foot to foot as if she'd caught Jackson's habit of perpetual motion.

'You won't.'

'How can you know? What if I go crashing into you and we both go flying?'

'Then we'll fake it.'

'Don't you get stage fright?'

'Of course I do. Like, so bad I want to be sick. That's why I learnt how to fake it!' He didn't look at Maeve as he spoke, and suddenly she realised he was as nervous as she was. But when the cymbals crashed and they tumbled out onto the stage, neither of them missed a beat.

The footlights were so bright that it was impossible to make out the faces of the people in the audience but Maeve knew Por Por and Goong Goong were out there. They'd flown down from Surfers Paradise especially for opening night. Andy would be sitting up in the Circle with Ned on his lap. Maeve put an extra spring in her step when she thought of how excited Ned would be when Andy told him that Maeve was that wild, bouncing, blue-haired Thing on stage.

At the end of the show, Maeve didn't want to leave the backstage area. She pulled off her blue wig and sat on the emergency exit stairs, looking down over the crowds of performers.

'Wasn't it brilliant?' said Bianca. 'Even if my part was so minuscule, this has been the best, best night of my life.'

'You were an awesome umbrella stand,' said Maeve.

'I thought Jackson was going to skewer me, the way he came flying across the stage with that umbrella like a spear. That guy must have ADD, he is so hyper.'

'But he's fun,' said Maeve.

'And cute, even if he is a short-arse. Go on, admit it. You think he's cute.'

Maeve stood up and stretched, ignoring her. 'I'd better get out of this costume. I've gotta catch Ned and Andy in the foyer and then meet my grandparents at the stage-door entrance. Keeping them apart is like serious politics.'

Ned squealed with excitement as Maeve pushed through the crowded foyer towards him. As soon as she drew close, he lunged through space, straight into her arms.

'You were incredible, Maeve,' said Andy. 'You and that other kid looked like you'd drunk rocket fuel.'

'Thanks, Andy,' said Maeve. 'Thanks for coming.'

'Do you want to come out for a hot chocolate to celebrate and then I'll drive you back to the boarding house?' he asked.

'I can't. They're waiting for me,' said Maeve, avoiding meeting his eyes. She didn't need to see his face to know his expression had grown cool.

'Well, I'll see you next Friday afternoon, then,' said Andy.

'I can't make it next Friday. We're doing a matinee for schools and there's an evening show too.'

'Right, I get it,' said Andy, taking Ned away from her.

'Don't be like that, Andy. I'll come the Friday after, I promise.'

'You do what you have to do, kid,' said Andy. He brushed his cheek against hers, a quick, perfunctory kiss, and Ned grabbed a handful of her hair. Then they were gone. Maeve pushed her way back through the crowd, suddenly feeling as if part of the thrill of the evening had seeped away.

In the dressing room, everyone was talking at once, elated at the success of the show. Maeve sat down in a quiet corner and stuffed her performance notes into her dance bag.

'Is everything all right, Maeve?' asked McCabe, noticing her sitting alone in the corner. 'Do you need a lift back to the boarding house?'

'No, it's okay. My grandparents are waiting for me.'

'Good, I'd like to meet them.'

Maeve frowned. Great. Just what she didn't need. She could imagine her grandparents' response to meeting one of her teachers. They'd probably start grilling McCabe about whether Maeve was keeping up with her homework.

Outside, the night air was warm and balmy. Por Por was standing by the stage door in the midst of a crowd of waiting parents. She looked small and alone beside the younger couples. As soon as she caught sight of Maeve, her face lit up with pride.

Maeve hugged her. 'Where's Goong Goong?' she asked. 'There's a teacher that wants to meet you both.'

'He's waiting in the car,' said Por Por, frowning. Suddenly, Maeve realised she could never second-guess her grandmother. Por Por obviously wasn't excited at the prospect of a parent–teacher interview in the street. 'Are you ready to come back to Potts Point with us? Have you got your things?'

Before Maeve could answer, McCabe was beside them.

'Mrs Kwong, I'm Colm McCabe. I teach Maeve drama and music at St Philomena's.'

'Colm?' said Por Por, her eyes widening. She let go of Maeve's hand and Maeve felt her heart sink. She hoped Por Por wasn't going to say something to embarrass them both.

McCabe looked uncomfortable too. 'Yes, ma'am. Colm McCabe,' he repeated.

'You don't recognise me, do you?'

McCabe looked confused. 'I don't believe we've met.'

Por Por laughed. 'Not for a long time. Pine Creek. 1956, I think that was the year. The last time I saw you. You've grown a lot and I'm probably not an inch taller!'

Maeve wanted to shrink inside herself with embarrassment. What was Por Por on about? But then McCabe's frown lifted and he gave a shout of laughter.

'Lily! Lily Yen Lin! I don't believe it!' He reached out and took hold of Por Por's hands and they stood staring at each other in amazement. Maeve found herself standing off to one side, feeling bewildered. She was glad Goong Goong wasn't around. She knew Goong Goong thought it was uncool to shake hands with another man's wife, and more than that, there was something embarrassing about two old people being so excited to see each other.

Por Por turned to Maeve and put an arm around her. 'Siu Siu, when I was younger than you are now, I used to play cat's cradle and hopscotch and chasey with your Mr McCabe! You wouldn't believe it, would you. Fifty years! Colm, I still feel like that little girl.'

'Maeve's so like you. I can see it now.' McCabe turned to Maeve. 'Your grandmother could kick higher than anyone I'd ever met.'

'Ummmm,' said Maeve in a small voice. Then she became aware of the fact that they were standing under the streetlight and nearly all the other parents had left.

McCabe pulled a piece of card out of his pocket and hurriedly scribbled on it. 'Here's my phone number at home and at work. There's a lot of catching up that we need to do. But most importantly, I wanted to talk to you about Maeve. She's a very talented young performer and I'd like her to be part of this year's drama tour to England and Ireland.'

'What?' said Maeve. This evening was getting weirder by the minute. 'But don't you have to be in Year 10?'

'Normally, yes. But we have a few spare places left this year.' He turned to Por Por. 'Bianca Storelli's parents are keen for her to participate and I thought Maeve would make a good addition to the group as well.'

In the car on the way back to the flat, Maeve leant forward so that she could see her grandparents' faces, trying to read their expressions as she explained about the drama tour, but Por Por simply looked at Goong Goong, as if, like Maeve, she was trying to read which direction the wind might be blowing.

'Acting, dancing,' he finally said in a low, stern voice. 'This isn't real work. This is grown-ups behaving like children. And a holiday, during the school year? What sort of studying is this? What would you learn from this trip?'

Maeve slumped back in her seat and folded her arms. She thought, 'Maybe I'd learn something that would really annoy you. Maybe I'd learn about my real father.'

24

Missing in action

Maeve wished the show could run for months. It seemed unbelievable that after one short week it could all be over. On closing night, Bianca ran from one end of the girls' dressing room to the other, getting everyone to sign her *Seussmania* T-shirt. Jackson stood outside the door, his blue wig in his hand, waving for Maeve to come and talk to him.

'Are you coming to the after-party?' he asked.

'I'm not allowed to go,' said Maeve. 'My grandparents didn't like the fact it was in a club in the city. They think I'm too young.'

'That's too bad,' said Jackson. He looked at the ground as he shifted from foot to foot.

'Is something the matter?' asked Maeve. She could tell he was feeling uncomfortable, that there was something he wanted to say but he couldn't find the words.

'I got you these,' he said, thrusting a small pink package into her hand. 'I was going to give them to you at the after-party, but if you're not coming . . .'

Maeve couldn't make him meet her eye. He kept his gaze down and scuffed the ground with his foot as she unwrapped the tiny gift. Inside the folds of pink tissue paper lay a pair of earrings, two red-and-blue miniature Things. She laughed out loud.

'These are great,' she said.

'Look at them closely.'

Maeve laid the Things on the palm of her hand and studied them. On the chest of each creature was a letter.

'M and J. You and me,' she said. 'They're beautiful.'

Jackson grinned at his shoes.

'I think you're really something, Maeve.'

Suddenly, Maeve realised she should thank him but she wasn't sure how. She leant forward and gave Jackson a quick hug and then stepped back. Why did it always feel as if there was a charge of static electricity in the air when she was close to him?

'Gotta go,' said Maeve. 'My friend Steph is waiting out front for me.'

When she was settled in the taxi with Steph, Maeve pushed her face against the glass, watching the other performers stream out of the theatre.

'Do you have to make it so obvious?' said Steph.

'What?'

'That you'd rather be with Bianca than with me. At least you two got to be in the show together.'

'You could have auditioned as well.'

'No I couldn't. I would have had to quit my job. I can hardly keep up with my homework as it is. And now you're going to Ireland without me too. It's so not fair.'

Maeve turned to her. 'I'm not going to Ireland. My

grandparents won't let me. And we're still the Three Musketeers, even if Bunka goes to Ireland without us. Nothing can change that.'

Back at the apartment, Maeve microwaved a packet of popcorn and they took the bowl into the guest room where Maeve stayed when her grandparents were in Sydney. They climbed into the big double bed and flicked on the television. Maeve was channel-surfing when Steph snatched the controls out of her hand.

'No, wait,' said Steph, flicking back to SBS.

'We don't want to watch the news,' said Maeve. 'It's gross.'

'But it was about Iraq. Something has happened in Iraq.'

'Something's always happening in Iraq.'

Then Maeve realised why Steph had flipped out. A group of Australian soldiers had been attacked by a suicide bomber. Steph began to tremble.

'That's Ben's unit. That's my brother's unit,' she said. 'I know it is.'

There wasn't any question of Steph staying the night. She wanted to go home straight away, to wait for the updates. She was angry that her parents hadn't told her what had happened, but mostly she was frightened.

'I'll drive you home, Stephanie,' said Goong Goong. 'Get your things.'

'Can I come too, Goong Goong? To keep Steph company.'

'If you must,' he replied.

'Of course I must,' thought Maeve. 'That's what friends do for each other.'

Steph and Maeve sat in the back seat of the car together but every time they passed under a streetlight, Maeve noticed Goong Goong was watching them in the mirror.

'Maeve tells me you work very hard at McDonald's, Stephanie, and that's why you weren't in the show.'

'Steph's even more into acting than I am,' said Maeve. 'She's really good. She's saving up to go on next year's drama trip.'

As soon as she'd said it, she bit her lip. Maybe Goong Goong would think it was flaky to want to be an actor.

'So you're working with a goal. To make money for the tour. I admire that sort of resourcefulness very much,' said Goong Goong.

Maeve felt Goong Goong's remark like a rebuke. It was as if she couldn't do anything that really pleased him.

'I was hoping to meet up with my brother in London,' said Steph. 'But now . . .' She leant forward and covered her face with her hands.

'Don't worry, Steph. Ben will be okay.'

'How can you know that?'

'Because one bad thing for the Musketeers is enough.'

'What if it's one bad thing for each of us?' whispered Steph.

On the ride home from Stephanie's, Goong Goong and Maeve didn't speak. It was as if they couldn't think of anything to say to each other without someone else there. Maeve wondered if it was like this when her mother was little. She thought about Will saying his father had held the family together after Will's mother died. All of a sudden, Maeve grew frightened at the idea that something might happen to Por Por and then there'd only be her and Goong Goong left, with this great gulf of silence between them. She was glad when they pulled into the apartment carpark.

Maeve was barely in the door again when Steph phoned in tears. For a minute, Maeve thought it was going to be bad news, but Steph was sobbing with relief. Everything was okay. When Steph's father had finally got through to the hospital, Ben had said he was injured but not badly. They were sending him back to London for R&R and there was nothing for his family to worry about.

'You were right, Maeve. My dad says all that super-stitious stuff about bad things happening in threes is dumb. He is such a rock, my dad.'

Maeve switched off her mobile phone and pulled the green notebook from her bedside table. She hadn't written in it since before the *Seussmania* audition. It opened up on the page with the picture of her father. Would he be a rock if she knew him? Her pen hovered over the page. She wanted to write something about him but she didn't know him well enough. She'd studied his letter from Nepal so many times that she could almost recite it, but there were no clues in it about who he really was.

Things I know about my father
My father's name is David Lee. He was born in Ireland.
He has a good memory, he can recite poetry, he can draw and he could make my mum laugh.
He doesn't know I exist.

Things I know about Jackson
His full name is Jackson Delaney Totafurno. He was
born in Melbourne but came to live in Sydney when he
was three. He is a great dancer, he can kick arse and
he can make me laugh. He thinks I'm really something.

Maeve laughed. 'Really something' didn't look very interesting when she wrote it down, but it had felt so good when Jackson said it. She wanted to keep thinking about Jackson, but the photo of her father kept staring up at her. If she looked at him for too long she felt as if she could disappear into the crazy man's eyes. He shouldn't matter to her. She had her grandparents, Ned and Andy, her friends, and now she even had Jackson. Why should it matter that she didn't know who her father was?

25

The real thing

McCabe had organised a barbecue in a park near his apartment in Coogee for the cast and crew of *Seussmania* along with their families. Goong Goong didn't want any of the Kwongs to go. He sat in front of the television with the remote, staring crossly at the screen. Maeve knew this wasn't the sort of fight he was going to win. Slowly, Maeve was starting to understand that when Por Por wanted something badly enough, she always had her way.

'Will you still be here when we get home?' asked Maeve.

Goong Goong made a cross, grunty sort of sound and ignored the question. His bags were by the front door, packed and ready to go for his flight to Melbourne.

'Goong Goong's flight is at seven, darling,' said Por Por, taking Maeve by the hand. 'But he'll be home in a few days.'

Por Por kissed him quickly on the top of his head before they left and Maeve waved. She still felt too shy of Goong Goong to kiss him goodbye.

As they drew the apartment door shut behind them, they both breathed a sigh of relief.

'Why is Goong Goong so grumpy?' asked Maeve.

'Goong Goong has worked very hard all his life. When he was a little boy in China, he had nothing. Now, the things he has, he wants to hang onto.'

'Like us?'

Por Por's face did that neat and annoying trick of closing over and she didn't reply. Her expression became so still that Maeve couldn't guess what she was thinking.

The park at Coogee was bathed in a warm, filtered light that shone gold on the dry grass. The Norfolk pines cast blue shadows like tiger stripes across the ground. Jackson did a series of handsprings, his body a blur in the soft sunset glow. Maeve followed, cartwheeling across the park in his wake. She loved the feel of her body in motion, the way the world turned for her as she spun. She was so caught in the movement that she didn't realise Jackson had changed direction until he jackknifed into her. They landed in a tangle of limbs in the sandy grass.

'Ow, that so hurt!' said Maeve, sitting up and rubbing her forehead.

'Sorry,' said Jackson, looking genuinely worried. He leant in close to Maeve and touched her lightly on the forehead, brushing a strand of hair away. Maeve laughed at the concern on his face.

'It's okay. I'm fine,' she said. 'How about you?'

'Fine,' he said, still frowning. He was looking at her so intently that Maeve wondered if she had something stuck on her face. She lifted one hand to brush her cheek but Jackson stopped her, holding her wrist gently. Then he leant forward and Maeve found herself leaning towards him too. It was as if there was a magnetic force, drawing them closer to each other until finally, she was kissing him, his lips warm against her own.

'Oi!' yelled Will. 'Cunning or what! Kick a girl in the face and then make your move!'

Maeve and Jackson leapt apart as if they'd been electrocuted. Will strode towards them across the yellow grass. He reached a hand down to each teenager and pulled them to their feet.

'Feeding time, wild things,' he said. He headed towards the picnic area, dragging them along behind him. Maeve saw the tattoos of Thing One and Thing Two peeking out from beneath his singlet top. She pointed at them and Jackson laughed. 'He loves us. That's why we're a pair of tatts on his back.'

'Too right,' said Will. 'You are a total Thing, not a human being.'

'What about me?' said Maeve, in mock offence. 'I was Thing Two!'

'You are a Warrior Princess occasionally disguised as a Thing, Maeve. There is a difference. He's the real Thing,' said Will over his shoulder.

'It's your fault. You are a bad influence, man,' yelled Jackson, wincing as Will twisted his wrist.

'Don't worry, little cuz. Your time will come. One day you will be a bad influence too,' said Will.

'My mum would freak if I turned out like you.'

Will turned around, tousled Jackson's hair and bowed to Maeve. 'Don't listen to the little arsehole,' said Will. 'He should be so lucky. His mum *adores* me.'

Maeve felt laughter bubbling inside her. She'd always thought that only girls knew how to tease each other like this, but Will and Jackson were better than Bianca and Steph in full flight.

The cast and crew were starting to gather like seagulls around picnic tables groaning with food. Bianca was flirting with a guy from Newtown Secondary who had done the lighting design for *Seussmania*. All around, people were laughing and loading their plates with food. A cool breeze swept across the sea and made the branches of the dark pines wave gently. Maeve wanted to laugh out loud. Life could feel so perfect.

McCabe was turning meat on the barbecue while Por Por stood beside him, holding a platter loaded high with sausages. Maeve watched them laughing at some private joke and suddenly understood why Goong Goong hadn't wanted them to come.

As she sat with Jackson, watching the last glow of sunlight fade from the surface of the ocean, she wanted to ask him about every girl he'd ever met before her, but she couldn't bring herself to shape the question. It would sound as if she was stalking him. It seemed everyone had lived secret lives and the only bits she ever got to see were on the surface of things.

Later, everyone helped carry the remnants of the barbecue up to McCabe's apartment above the beach. Maeve heard the annoying tinkle of Por Por's phone ringing out over the cheerful conversations.

'I hate my gran's mobile tone,' she said to Jackson. 'It's so loud. Everyone always turns and checks us out when it rings. And she shouts into it, as if she can't believe such a little phone can work.'

Jackson laughed. 'Well, at least she uses one. Uncle Mac

won't touch them. He is so techno-phobic.'

As they pushed their way into the crowded living room, Jackson touched her hand lightly and she felt a rush of warmth shoot up her arm and make her cheeks glow. It was only when she caught sight of Por Por that she felt the warmth ebb. Por Por stood on the balcony with McCabe, her face pale, eyes wide, clutching her mobile. McCabe had an arm around her, as if to steady her.

'Por Por,' said Maeve, stepping forward. 'What is it? What's wrong?'

'It's your grandfather. He's had a heart attack. On the flight to Melbourne. He's in hospital. We have to go to him. We have to go now.'

26

A gift of the heart

They took a plane to Melbourne that night. At first, Por Por tried to argue that Maeve would have to go back to St Philomena's but Maeve couldn't bear the idea. What if she never had the chance to see Goong Goong again?

As soon as they walked onto the white, bleak ward, Maeve had the same sinking feeling she'd had that terrible day at St Vincent's. Goong Goong looked so shrunken, attached to tubes and machines that monitored his heart and breathing. He was heavily sedated and didn't even know they were standing beside him. Maeve stared at his prone figure while Por Por spoke quietly with the doctor. Goong Goong was out of danger. They needed to have a good night's sleep and come back to the hospital in the morning. There was nothing they could do.

For a long time, Maeve lay awake worrying about Goong Goong. Every time the fridge in their hotel room rumbled, Por Por sighed, so Maeve knew she couldn't sleep either. The night seemed to last forever.

Why had she insisted on coming to Melbourne? It wasn't as if it made any difference to Goong Goong. Sometimes she wondered if he'd let her go to boarding school just to get rid of her. She knew her mother had been a disappointment, and already he seemed to disapprove of every choice that Maeve made. It was her fourteenth birthday on Thursday and none of her friends would be around to help her celebrate. Why did she want to please him so badly? Why did she feel so frightened of losing him?

The next day, Por Por and Maeve spent the morning at the hospital. Maeve hated the stark, bare waiting room but she fought down her distress and stayed close to her grandmother. Por Por looked as if someone had sucked out all her energy. She sat clutching the cup of tea that Maeve had brought, her brow lined with anxiety.

'Can't they tell us when he'll wake up?' asked Maeve.

'Some time this afternoon, perhaps,' said Por Por wearily.

'Por Por, you can't wait around here like this all day. It's not doing you any good and it's not helping Goong Goong. Why don't we go for a walk? You've got your mobile. They'll call if he needs you.'

Por Por didn't answer. She wrinkled her nose in distaste as she sniffed the tea before setting it down on a table. Then she fumbled in her handbag, searching for something.

'Your Mr McCabe gave me the address of a restaurant that a friend of his owns. It's not far. Some good tea, that would help us both.'

At the Golden Phoenix restaurant, Por Por asked the maître d if Mr Keith Kwong was available. Within minutes, a man in a stylish, tailored black suit and a pale blue tie made his way towards them. His face was lined but his hair was still jet-black with only a hint of silver at the temples. He bowed slightly to Por Por and smiled at Maeve.

'I'm sorry we have to meet under such unfortunate circumstances, Madame Kwong. Colm phoned and explained your situation. If there's anything I can do to help, please feel free to call upon me.'

'Thank you. You're too kind. Good tea would be very soothing,' said Por Por.

After he'd gone, Por Por pulled out her mobile phone and stared at it, as if willing it to ring.

'Call the hospital for me, Siu Siu,' she said, handing Maeve her phone. 'Perhaps they have forgotten my phone number.'

Obediently, Maeve dialled the number, asked for the nurse on Goong Goong's ward and then handed the phone to Por Por. Maeve could tell by the look on her grandmother's face that there was no news.

'We could be in Melbourne days or weeks. What will your Mr McCabe think of you missing so much school?'

'The school will be fine about it, Por Por. Don't worry.'

'But your Mr McCabe is probably wondering about Goong Goong too. We should call him.'

'There's nothing to tell him yet. And please stop calling him *my* Mr McCabe!' said Maeve. 'He's your friend. He's only my teacher.'

'*Jun see jong dou!*' scolded Por Por.

'What's that mean?'

'It means your teachers are precious and must be respected. Respect for your teachers, respect for the past – these things are important, Siu Siu. If you don't honour the past, the ghosts can come back to haunt you. Haven't I told you that before? Hungry ghosts are spirits that haven't been honoured.'

Suddenly, they both realised that Keith Kwong and a waiter with a tray of tea things were standing at their table. Maeve blushed. Por Por had never scolded her in front of strangers. Keith looked from Maeve to her grandmother.

'Perhaps what both you ladies need is some distraction from your worries,' he said. 'I have another restaurant in Williamstown. It's a beautiful drive over the West Gate Bridge. Please, let me give you a small tour and be my guests for lunch. You must see Williamstown. That's real old Melbourne. Colm and I lived there when we were kids.'

Keith Kwong's restaurant in Williamstown overlooked the blue-grey waters of Port Phillip Bay. Maeve watched the colour flood back into Por Por's cheeks as she ate. Even though they only managed to eat a small amount, the food was so delicious that they both felt more optimistic.

As they drove along the waterfront on their way back to the city, Maeve looked at the sea wistfully. Her body ached to be in motion. She hated the thought of having to return to the confines of the hospital waiting room.

'Could we go for a walk along the beach before we go back, please?' she asked.

'Sounds like a great idea to me,' said Keith.

Por Por shut her eyes, her face drawn with tiredness. 'Perhaps I'll wait for you here.'

Keith parked in a quiet spot so they could walk along the foreshore while Por Por napped in the car. Maeve tucked her hair behind her ears and put her head down into the wind. When a bad squall moved in across the water, they both broke into a run. Ahead, a lump of rock stood in the middle of the grassy strand. It was barely big enough to shelter the two of them.

'Sorry about this!' shouted Keith above the wind.

'It's okay. I like it. Besides, it was my idea.'

Maeve turned and touched the bronze plaque set into the rock.

'What is this thing?'

'I think they call it the Famine Rock.'

Maeve read the inscription. 'It says they put it up for the 150th anniversary of the Irish famine. It says Irish orphan girls landed here. I wish I could go there – Ireland, I mean.'

Keith laughed. 'Ireland before China?'

'I'm just as Irish as I am Chinese. I mean – I'm not either, really. I'm Aussie.'

'That's the way I used to feel. But if you travel, you wind up carrying pieces of everywhere inside you like long-lost loves. You know, when I go to China now, when I see the lights of Hong Kong harbour, I feel the same sort of excitement that I feel when the plane circles over Port Phillip Bay. It's as if I have two homes, two hearts, two languages.'

'I've only got one of everything,' said Maeve. She glanced over at the car, suddenly worried. Por Por was holding her mobile phone, frowning at the keypad.

'I think we should be getting back to the hospital,' said Maeve. Suddenly she felt frightened that she might have only one grandparent.

Shortly before dinner, Maeve and Por Por were finally allowed in to see Goong Goong. He was sitting up in bed watching television and looking tired, but he smiled when they came into the room. After ten minutes of stilted conversation, Por Por left to buy Goong Goong something from Chinatown for his evening meal. They'd both decided the hospital food was inedible.

'I'll come and help,' said Maeve.

'No, you must mind your Goong Goong,' said Por Por. 'I won't be long.'

Maeve sat down on the chair beside the bed and she and Goong Goong silently watched the evening news.

Suddenly Goong Goong offered the remote to Maeve. 'Would you like to be in charge?' he asked.

'That's okay, Goong Goong. I'll watch whatever you want to watch.'

But Goong Goong switched the TV off and turned to gaze at Maeve.

'So we will talk instead,' he said.

Maeve felt a tightness in her chest. She and Goong Goong never talked about anything. She fumbled around in her memory, trying to think of something to say that he might find interesting. But she didn't know anything about banks or business or the stock market or any of the things he probably thought were good to talk about. She took a breath, but no words emerged.

'It's your birthday on Thursday,' he said. 'Fourteen years old this week. Have you thought what you might like for a birthday gift?'

Maeve didn't know how to answer. She was surprised Goong Goong even remembered when her birthday was. He'd never even signed the birthday cards that Por Por had sent over the years.

'Ummm. Not really,' she said.

'Well, I have been thinking of this problem.'

He gestured to the drawer beside the bed and Maeve pulled it open.

'Could you find me my wallet, Siu Siu. They've taken out all my cards and all my money and put them in the safe deposit. But there is something very valuable that I have kept which I believe is very precious. I want to show you.'

Maeve took out her grandfather's shiny black leather wallet. She noticed how smooth it was as she handed it to him.

He frowned as he pulled open the compartments and looked inside.

'Ah, here it is.'

It was a tiny scrap of paper folded in half. Silently he handed it to Maeve. When she unfolded it, she saw it was a page torn from a desk diary: 17 March 1991, the day Maeve was born.

'I've carried it with me since that day. A most auspicious date, don't you agree?'

Maeve smiled and looked at the slip of paper in awe. She tried to imagine her grandfather at his desk when the phone call came through that she had been born, carefully removing the date from his desk calendar and putting it in his wallet. On the bottom of the page, a quote for the day was printed in tiny letters: *The joys of parents are secret, and so are their griefs and fears. Francis Bacon, 1561–1626.*

Maeve folded the slip of paper into a neat square again and put it back in the wallet.

'Thanks, Goong Goong,' she said.

Goong Goong reached out to her and for a minute she thought he simply wanted the paper back, but he took her hand and clasped it in both of his.

'I think, for your fourteenth birthday, I would like to give you and your friend Stephanie a gift. I believe a gift you can share with your friend will give the most pleasure. So I would like for you both to go on this trip that your teacher proposed. My gift to you, Maeve.'

Maeve felt her eyes sting with tears. 'You don't have to do that, Goong Goong. You just have to get better. That will be a really good present.'

'No. I'm still the person in charge around here and I say you and Stephanie will go on this drama tour. Okay?'

Maeve laughed through her tears. 'Okay, Goong Goong. You're still the boss.'

27

Guilty secrets

On the morning of Maeve's fourteenth birthday, Por Por put her in a taxi to the airport. Goong Goong and Por Por would be following in a few more days but they both wanted Maeve to get back to Sydney in time to celebrate her birthday with her friends. As the taxi tried to cross one of the main streets, it was stopped by police who were holding up traffic while a parade meandered past. A slow-moving truck nudged along the wide main street. It was decorated in green and Maeve caught a glimpse of a green and gold banner. On the back of the truck, sitting on a throne, was a man with a long white beard wearing green and gold robes and holding a bishop's mitre.

'Is that the St Patrick's Day Parade?' Maeve asked the taxi-driver.

'St Patrick's Day?' echoed the driver, mystified. But Maeve knew she was right. She leant out the window and watched the parade pass by.

Following the truck was a troupe of Irish dancers in traditional costume twirling ribbons as if they were straight out of *Riverdance*. In the midst of the youngest dancers was a small Asian girl. Beside the freckle-faced blonde and red-headed dancers, she looked oddly out of place. Would Maeve be out of place in Ireland? If she found her father, would he expect her to become part of his life? She felt a guilty shiver at the thought of him. To search for her father when Goong Goong had been the one to make her journey possible felt like a betrayal.

Steph couldn't believe that Goong Goong had offered to pay her way. At first her parents weren't keen for her to accept, but when she argued that it meant she'd be able to see Ben and that if she didn't go Maeve might not be allowed, they relented. The trip was to fall across part of the first-term break and one week of second term.

On a cool autumn night a week before they were to depart, Maeve pushed a chair up against the door of the bedroom she shared with Viv. She needed to dance without being interrupted. The music from the portable CD player sounded tinny in the boarding-house bedroom, but she didn't care. The song was 'Blue and Yellow' by The Used, and it suited her mood. She wanted to dance until she didn't feel anything but the rhythm of the music filling every corner of her mind.

When Gina banged on the thin partition wall, Maeve turned off the CD player and sat on the floor, annoyed. There were so many thoughts she couldn't sort through, so much thwarted energy rippling under her skin. She hated feeling this way. When her mobile rang, she didn't even notice who was calling.

'Yes,' she snapped. She knew she sounded angry.

'Is that Maeve?'

'Oh, hey,' she said, taken aback. 'Hey, Jackson.'

'You want to waste some time with me?'

Maeve laughed. 'That's a line from "Blue and Yellow". Have you been listening to The Used?'

'Umm, yeah,' said Jackson shyly, his cover blown.

'That is weird. I love that band. And I was just listening to them too.'

'Well, I don't know what the hell that means. But I guess maybe you should meet me after school tomorrow. Maybe. Because, like, if you want to. Or whatever.' His words came out in a rush, as if he were racing to get them said as quickly as possible.

'Okay,' said Maeve. 'Where?'

'Can you meet me at Central?'

'Why Central?'

'There's a photo booth there. I thought it would be cool to get a pic of you and me before you go to Ireland. You know, one where we don't have blue wigs on.'

Maeve laughed. It would be tricky to go without getting permission, but Central wasn't too far away. She could probably get there and back before anyone noticed she was missing.

When she switched off the mobile, she felt as if all the restless energy had settled in her chest like a cloud of butterflies but this time it was a good feeling, a feeling that she wanted to hold onto.

Jackson was lounging against the side of the photo booth in a pair of low-slung jeans and an oversized windcheater, his skateboard tucked under one arm. Maeve had changed out of her school uniform but suddenly she wished she'd put on something different. The strap on her favourite singlet top was broken and she'd had to use a safety pin to hold it in place. Her black jeans suddenly felt too tight and the daisies on her thongs looked babyish.

As soon as Jackson saw her, he dropped his board and skated towards her.

''S'up, Warrior Princess?' he said. He smiled at Maeve as if she really was a princess and he was ecstatic at the prospect of meeting her. Suddenly, what she was wearing didn't matter one little bit.

They squashed into the photo booth, laughing at the simple pleasure of being alone together. There were four buttons to choose from, each offering different photo options. First up they tried the option that produced four different photos, but somehow they managed to both look goofy in every frame. Either Jackson was looking down so you only saw the cowlick on the top of his head or Maeve had her eyes shut.

'If we just act natural we could get a good photo,' said Maeve.

'Okay, but I'll have to be kissing you just as the flash goes,' said Jackson.

'That sounds way too dangerous,' said Maeve. 'Why don't we try being ourselves?'

They put their arms around each other's shoulders and stared into the lens. Maeve could feel energy surging through them both as Jackson hit the button. It wasn't until after the flash had fired that he turned to kiss her.

The photos were perfect. Their heads were tilted towards each other and they were both smiling. They looked like best friends. As they sat in Subway sharing a vegetarian sub, Maeve opened out her green notebook and slipped her strip of four tiny photos inside.

'Is that your diary?' asked Jackson.

'Sort of. It used to belong to my mum. I keep all sorts of stuff inside it.'

'Secret stuff?'

'Yeah, secret stuff,' said Maeve.

'Like what?'

'It wouldn't be secret if I told you! Stuff about my life and my friends and my mum and dad. Ordinary stuff.'

'There is nothing ordinary about you, Kwong. Absolutely nothing you tell me could be a surprise.'

Maeve looked into Jackson's laughing brown eyes. She took a deep breath, flipped the notebook open on the page with the photos of her father and turned them around so Jackson could see. She told him everything she knew, showed him the Weaving Girl and talked about what going to Ireland could mean.

'I haven't even told Steph and Bianca,' said Maeve, taking back the notebook. 'I feel really guilty not sharing it with them. We've always told each other everything. But I'm scared that if I tell them, then they'll pressure me to do something. I'm not sure what I want to do. Not yet. So it's like the biggest secret. You can't tell anyone.'

Jackson leant across the table. For a moment, Maeve thought he was going to kiss her. But instead, he gently adjusted the strap of her singlet top, snibbing the safety pin shut. Then he brushed her long fringe away from her eyes. 'Your secrets are safe with me,' he whispered.

When Maeve got back to the boarding house, she sat

down on the bed and pulled the green notebook out of her bag. She flipped through it, searching for a blank page to paste in the photos of Jackson and herself. The notebook was so much thicker now, the pages buckling with the number of images that were glued inside it. She turned back to where her father's letter was pasted down and smoothed out the ripples of the thin onionskin paper. She squirmed as she read through the first romantic paragraph. This guy was definitely hot for her mother. Why had he disappeared? There was no return address, no indication of where he was heading next or if he'd ever return to Ireland. Maeve looked at the tiny photo-booth image again, studying every crevice of his face. She picked up a pen and began to write in tiny letters around the margins of the page.

Who is David Lee? Is he still alive? Why did my grandparents hate him? Why did he leave Mum? Why didn't Mum tell me every secret little thing about him? Why does it matter to me? What if I did find him and he was horrible? Or if he was perfect? A perfect dad who had always wanted a daughter? What if he asked me to stay?

The next morning, as soon as she could get into the school library, Maeve googled Davy Lee. She groaned when the results came up. Four million and forty thousand! She changed it to David Lee but that got even more results – more than a hundred million sites popped up in the Google listing. It was a name that everyone owned. There were millions of Chinese Lees and millions of Anglo-Irish Lees all around the world. She'd always known it was a common Chinese name but never realised the world was full of Irish Lees as well. Why couldn't he have been called something unusual, something unique that would make it possible to find him?

The first Davy Lee that had shown up owned a business selling caravans. Another was an old movie star. It was hopeless. She didn't have any clues. She flipped open the green notebook and frowned at the drawings on his letter. The bell for first period was going to ring soon and she'd have to come back and try again later.

Frantically, she tried adding all sorts of different key words; 'Ireland', 'Nepal', and finally, as a wild guess, 'artist'. Finally, she got the results down to one million hits. Her dad was one in a million. How was she ever going to find him? Should she even be trying?

Goong Goong and Por Por arranged to be in Sydney the day before Maeve was to fly overseas. Maeve let herself into the Potts Point apartment. Her bags were waiting for her, neatly stacked beside the bed in the spare room. She sat down at the end of her bed and stared at the suitcases. They didn't look out of place. It made her realise she'd been living out of a suitcase ever since her mother had died. Nowhere felt like home any more.

That night at dinner, Por Por outdid herself cooking Maeve's favourite dishes: pan-fried dumplings, steamed fish with coriander and chilli, and crunchy Chinese greens with oyster sauce. Maeve had got used to not talking while they ate, so she was surprised when Goong Goong turned to her and said, 'Siu Siu, this journey, it will change you.

There is a Chinese proverb I would like you to think about while you are away. "A tree has its roots, a stream its source." Do you understand this saying?'

'Sort of,' said Maeve, rolling her chopsticks between her fingers. Was he asking her to be grateful for his generosity or was he warning her against something?

Goong Goong still wasn't well enough to drive, so Steph's parents picked Maeve up from Potts Point the next morning for the trip out to the airport. Por Por hugged Maeve extra tight, holding onto her as if it was the last time they would see each other.

'It's okay, Por Por. I'll be back in a few weeks,' said Maeve.

'I know. But it's a long way. You take care. Stay close to Mr McCabe and the other girls. Don't go anywhere alone.'

It was a relief to get all the baggage checked and finally make it to the gates of international departures. Girls were hugging their parents goodbye and kissing their boyfriends as McCabe and Ms Donahue did a head count and checked that everyone was ready. The St Philomena's girls were about to pass through the barrier where family and friends couldn't follow when Andy came running towards them, dodging Ned's pusher between the crowds. The wheels squealed as he came to a violent stop beside Maeve.

'May-yay!' shouted Ned, reaching out for her.

'Maeve, I'm sorry we're late. We were just about to go when Ned pulled a cup of chocolate milk all over himself and I had to change his clothes.'

'You could have brought him sticky. I wouldn't have minded,' said Maeve.

She held Ned in her arms and squashed his face close to hers. It made her eyes prick with tears. Awkwardly, Andy hugged her too, enveloping Ned at the same time.

'Maeve,' he whispered. 'I'm sorry for all the crap that's gone down lately. Ned is my only son but you're my only daughter. You can come home to us. Any time. When you're ready. You can always come home to us. One day, any day.'

Maeve pressed her face against Ned's tummy, needing to hide.

'Thanks, Andy,' she mumbled, and handed Ned back.

She scooped up her flight bag and followed the other girls through the doors without looking back.

28

Ghost world

Even though Maeve had been in airports more times than she could count, she'd never passed through the doors to international departures. It was like entering another world, a weird holding bay between universes. There were backpackers and businessmen, whole families with sleepy children draped over the parents' shoulders, and the excited gaggle of St Philomena's students clustered together in the queue. Ms Donahue stood at the front, clutching the passports and then handed one to each of the girls as they approached the customs checkpoint.

Bianca looked bored. She'd been through this routine too many times. Then a security guard opened her bag for inspection.

'But they're only tweezers,' said Bianca, looking outraged that anything of hers should be confiscated. 'You know, you pluck your eyebrows with them!'

'Sorry, miss. No sharp objects on board. That's the rules.'

Bianca turned to Maeve and muttered angrily, 'Oh what, like I'm so going to hijack a plane with a pair of tweezers. What do they think I'm going to do? Pluck the air hostess to death? I mean, pleeeze.'

Steph sighed. 'I'll just be glad when we're on the plane. I won't believe we've made it out of Australia until we touch down in Hong Kong.'

It was a nine-hour flight but between the meals, the movies and the endless swapping of seats, the hours disappeared quickly.

Maeve pressed her face against the glass as they descended. She gripped the arms of her seat so tightly that Steph turned to her.

'What's wrong? Are you scared of the landing?'

'No, I'm thinking. About Mum. How I always thought I'd come here with her one day. And now I'm here without her.'

Steph slipped her hand over Maeve's and held it tight. 'But you're not alone, Maeve.'

Hong Kong was warm and steamy. The minibus hummed with the excited conversation of girls as it drove along Nathan Road. It was dark by the time they reached the hotel in Kowloon but no one was tired.

'It's stupid being in Hong Kong first,' said Bianca. 'We should be coming here on the way home so we can shop.'

Maeve shrugged. 'It's just meant to break the flight, Bunka. It's a drama tour, not a shopping tour.'

'They'd better let us at least go to the night markets.'

Maeve glanced at their itinerary. 'We're doing that tonight. Looks like we've got something to do every minute of the day tomorrow as well. Por Por gave me this long list of relatives she wanted me to try and contact but we've only got twenty-four hours.'

Ms Donahue and McCabe marshalled the girls into

small groups and they headed out into the warm, oily night. Everything about Hong Kong surprised Maeve; the brilliant colours of the neon signs in Nathan Road, the hazy swirl of exhaust fumes mingling with the rich layers of cooking scents exuded by the roadside foodstalls, the bustle of millions of people all hurrying into the night, talking, laughing, intent upon their evening business. People turned to stare at Maeve, taking a second look at the pale-skinned Asian girl walking arm-in-arm with two fair-haired Australians. She'd noticed that reaction to her before in Chinatown, the way some people would turn back to look at her, trying to decide if she was an Asian-looking white girl or a Western-looking Asian girl. She listened to the sound of their voices, the way the words seemed to have a strange lilt to them that went up and down like notes in a song. She made a vow to herself that one day she really would go to Chinese school and learn how to speak the language.

McCabe stuck close to the Musketeers as they were jostled by the crowds along Temple Street.

'Are you shadowing us, sir?' asked Bianca.

'You three are the youngest students on the tour,' said McCabe.

'Oh, I thought you were hoping to pick up some tips on how to bargain,' said Bianca.

She stopped at a trestle table laden with old Chinese coins, Communist Party badges and antique-looking chess sets. There were even old wind-up alarm clocks with the face of Mao Zedong nodding in time to the second hand.

'Omar would love one of these,' said Bianca, picking up one of the alarm clocks.

'Omar?' said Steph and Maeve in unison.

'I know. He was a jerk. But he's matured.'

Bianca held the clock up and the stall-holder keyed a price into his calculator and showed it to her.

'*Ho gwai!*' she exclaimed, shaking her head.

The stall-holder tried another amount but Bianca held out until, sighing, he reduced it to a quarter of the original price.

Maeve felt embarrassed that she didn't know what *ho gwai* meant. She was glad when Bianca explained to McCabe that it was Chinese for 'too expensive'.

As they moved deeper into the markets, Maeve kept imagining she caught a glimpse of someone she knew weaving through the crowd. Every few minutes, a voice would make her start, as if someone had spoken her name, as if they were quietly calling her. But when she spun around to try and discover who it was, she was confronted by a sea of strangers. She quickened her pace and kept close to Bianca and Steph.

When they reached the Tin Hau Temple, Steph was excited to find a row of fortune-tellers. While Steph went to have her fortune told, Bianca haggled with a stall-holder. Maeve glanced over her shoulder again. The feeling wouldn't go away. It was as if someone was stalking her, but not someone evil. She was sure it was someone she knew. Suddenly, it dawned on her who it was. Every woman behind every stall, every figure disappearing into the shadows seemed to hold an echo of her mother. She stood very still and let the feeling possess her. A wave of déjà vu swept over her.

'Are you all right, Maeve?' asked McCabe. His voice pulled her back from the edge of darkness.

'I didn't expect to feel like this,' she said.

'Are you jet-lagged?'

'No,' said Maeve. 'It's as if I'm being haunted, but not in a bad way. I have this weird feeling that I've been here before.'

'Some people believe that we carry our ancestors' memories with us, even if we never knew them,' said McCabe. 'They call it race memory.'

Maeve nodded. Her heart felt too full for her to speak. She could see Goong Goong here as a young man, she could see Por Por and her mother visiting as mother and daughter. Goong Goong's proverb came back to her: 'A tree has its roots, a stream its source.' Was this the source of her family? She shut her eyes and let the feeling of belonging wash over her.

The next morning, they caught the subway down to the Star Ferry Terminal from their hotel in Kowloon so they could cross over to Hong Kong Island.

'It's like being in Sydney,' said Steph, as they stepped onto the ferry.

The roar of the ferry engine, the lapping of the waters against the prow, the sharp tang of oil and salt, made Maeve feel at home. The sense of belonging that she'd felt at the night markets was even stronger here. The Star Ferry chugged across the wide harbour in exactly seven minutes and the tribe of St Philomena's girls marched across the terminal to where trams shot up the side of Victoria Peak, the highest point in Hong Kong.

When they reached the Peak they could see right across the island and the harbour to the New Territories. The girls all squashed up close as a group while Bianca took photos with her digital camera. She was the only one with global roaming on her mobile, so everyone wanted her to send snapshots home. While she was busy being the official photographer, Maeve leant on the railing and gazed out at the view.

A dense smog sat like heavy cloud between the sky-scrapers. The side of the peak was thick with lush tropical growth, and the city leapt out of the space between the water and the forest like a dream of glass and steel.

In that moment, Maeve felt it again – as if her mother was behind her. A breeze swirled up the side of the Peak and blew Maeve's hair from her face. She shut her eyes, holding the moment, imagining Sue really was beside her, not a shimmering ghost but real and warm and alive again. When she opened her eyes, she felt surrounded and yet utterly alone. It was the weirdest feeling. The other girls had all left the viewing deck and the wind had suddenly become sharp. She stared down at the haze of pollution that blanketed the city, trying to make sense of her emotions.

'Maeve!' called McCabe, startling her from her reverie. 'You're not quite with us, are you?'

'Sorry, sir. I didn't think that being here would mean anything. But I keep having all these weird feelings. There's a lot I have to figure out about this place.'

'I'm afraid you'll have to save that for another trip. We really need to keep moving.'

Maeve smiled. 'That's okay, sir. I'm definitely coming back here one day. The ghosts can wait until then.'

29

Secret-keeper

Maeve glanced across at McCabe as they stood waiting for their bus outside Dublin Airport. Sometimes she felt he was watching her, as if he knew she was planning something. She wished she didn't feel so edgy. It wasn't as if she was likely to bump into David Lee on the first street corner. She wouldn't even recognise him if she did. But as the bus moved into the traffic, she pressed her face against the glass, trying to take in every sight and sound of Dublin, wondering if he was out there somewhere.

Rain sleeted down as the mini-bus pulled up outside their accommodation. The B&B was a tall Victorian terrace house with six steps up to a shiny black front door. Maeve, Bianca and Stephanie dragged their suitcases up a narrow flight of stairs lined with fading line drawings of the sights of Dublin. The whole building smelt faintly of bacon, but it was warm and cosy in their room at the top. The ceiling sloped down on all sides and Bianca insisted they toss a coin to see who shared the double bed and who won the only single.

'I hate that carpet. That's the sort of carpet that used to give me nightmares when I was little. You know, you look over the side of the bed and the swirly bits look like giant spiders.'

'What are you worrying about the carpet for?' said Maeve. 'We're in Dublin! This is where the tour really starts. This is where things are going to happen!'

Maeve hurried over to the window to look out into the street. They were near a canal in a long line of terraces. Maybe her father was just around the corner. Maybe her whole life was about to change.

In the morning, they were served huge plates of fried eggs with bacon, tomatoes and something that looked like a dark sliced sausage.

'What's this?' asked Bianca, prodding the speckled circle of meat.

'It's black pudding,' said McCabe, amused.

'Black pudding?'

'It's traditional. They make it with blood, that's why it's so dark,' he said.

Every girl in the breakfast room pushed the little dark circles to the corner of their plates except Maeve.

'Black pudding is no big deal. My granny makes me eat pig's blood *congee*. If I can handle Chinese food, I can handle Irish. I mean, I am half-Irish.'

'Well, so am I,' said Steph. 'Like, all my ancestors came from Ireland, but that doesn't mean I have to regress!'

After breakfast they met in the street. There was a bite in the spring air and Maeve plunged her hands deep into her pockets.

Ms Donahue handed out copies of the day's itinerary plus a list of emergency procedures. On the back was a map of how to get back to the B&Bs if they got separated from the group. Maeve slipped the sheet into her pocket. She was definitely going to be separated from everyone and she couldn't wait. She had her own plans.

As they walked along the streets of Dublin, Maeve found herself looking into the faces of the crowd, searching for a man with pale eyes and wild hair, a scary ghost of a man who might be her father. She turned at the familiar sound of a voice but it was only an Australian tourist. Of course her dad wouldn't sound Australian. No, he'd have a soft Irish accent and he'd look much older than the face in the photo. But the more she searched the crowds, the more daunting her task became. The faces on the street were young, with pink cheeks, not the weathered face she imagined her father would possess. The only older people seemed to be the beggars on the footpaths. A man lying asleep in a doorway caught her eye. What if she pulled back the green chenille bedspread covering his face and discovered her father? The possibility sent a chill down her spine.

In O'Connell Street, they boarded a double-decker tour bus. 'It's a good way for you all to get your bearings, girls,' announced Ms Donahue, as the bus wove its way through the streets of Dublin.

'It's a good way to freeze our arses off,' said Bianca, pulling the collar of her coat up high. It started to rain and most of the girls went below, but Steph and Maeve stuck it out on the open roof of the red double-decker.

Maeve noted where everything was, as if she was soaking up a map of the city, soaking it into her bones. As the bus drove past the General Post Office she sat up and craned to see it.

'And in 1916, the post office was the site of the famous

Easter uprising that turned the tide against the English,' said the guide.

'I read about that!' said Steph, turning to Maeve in her excitement. 'This is so cool. It's all, like, weirdly familiar. My great-great-grandparents came from Ireland. It's sort of like finding my roots, seeing all this.'

'McCabe told me there's this theory that people can remember their ancestors' past,' said Maeve.

Steph nodded, as if she could believe it was possible. 'Where is McCabe?' she asked.

'I don't know. I haven't seen him since breakfast,' said Maeve. She flicked open her guidebook and put a star next to the post office. That could be a good place to start a search for her father. Then she felt a flash of doubt. What if she actually found him?

As the morning passed, Maeve started to worry she'd never be able to separate herself from the group. Ms Donahue was constantly counting students. There were only fifteen of them and Maeve was the youngest and the only Asian-looking girl. Having her own agenda could be a serious problem.

After the bus trip, they walked to Trinity College for their second tour of the morning.

'When can we go shopping?' whispered Bianca.

Steph smiled. 'Hang in there, Bunka. Just a little bit more culture and then you can start spending that fistful of euros.'

Inside the College's Long Library, bookshelves rose up to a dark, vaulted timber ceiling, and thin spring sunshine shone through elongated windows onto the wooden floors. Long ladders ran from the floor to the top shelves. In a room beyond, a special darkened cell housed an ancient book called 'The Book of Kells'.

'It's incredible. It's so old, so precious,' said Steph.

'Who cares,' said Bianca, flipping through her guide-book, searching for the shopping district.

Steph was about to launch into a defensive rant but Maeve stopped her and turned to Bianca. 'Don't do that, Bunka.'

'What?'

'Dis all the important bits. The past is important.'

'Not to me, it isn't,' said Bianca. 'Now is what matters.'

'If you didn't know that your grandfather was from Italy, if you didn't know who your mum or your dad was, if you didn't know who *you* really were, maybe you'd understand.'

Maeve hadn't meant to sound so fierce. Even Steph was staring at her, startled by her outburst.

'Um, yeah, that's what I think too,' added Steph uncertainly.

When the tour finished, the girls were allowed to go off in twos and threes to shop. The Musketeers headed for Grafton Street, the bustling centre of the shopping area.

Maeve felt as if her feet were dragging as she followed her friends. She needed to get back to the post office on her own. They zigzagged up and down the streets of Dublin until they found themselves walking through Temple Bar, a tangle of tiny side streets near the Liffey River. Suddenly, Maeve realised the post office was just the other side of the river.

'Hey look,' said Bianca. 'It's an Internet café. Let's send some emails home.'

'There was something in that shop around the corner that I wanted to look at again,' said Maeve.

'We'll come with you,' said Steph.

'No, it's cool. I'll only be a minute. You get started on your emails. If we get separated, I'll meet you back at the B&B,' she called over her shoulder as she ran down the cobbled laneway.

A steady rain started to fall as she crossed O'Connell Bridge. The traffic was thick and for a minute, Maeve found herself stranded under a tall statue of an Irish politician. She wrapped her arms tightly around herself and shivered as she watched for a break in the stream of cars and buses.

Inside the General Post Office there were long queues waiting to use the phones. A polished wooden bench ran along one wall, with stacks of phone books slotted into the shelves above it. Maeve pulled out a Dublin directory and flipped through to the letter L. But when she found the page for 'Lee', her heart sank. There were hundreds of Lees in Dublin alone. Any one of them might be her relative, but she couldn't possibly phone them all.

She stood in the colonnaded entrance to the post office and stared out at the rain. It was so frustrating. Maybe he was still in Nepal. Or maybe he was living just around the corner. She'd counted twelve David Lees and three D. Lees in the Dublin directory alone, and there was a directory for every county. How many were there in all Ireland, and which one was her father? As she turned to walk away, she was startled to realise McCabe was standing only metres away from her, hunched over a pay phone as if he was a spy intent on a secret mission. Maeve hurried away.

She couldn't afford for him to see her alone.

She stopped on the bridge and leant over to stare into the dark waters of the Liffey. Had her father ever stood here and wondered about her mother? She tried to conjure him in her imagination but nothing came. He didn't haunt her like the memory of her mother. Maybe that was a good thing, maybe that meant he was still alive.

By the time she made her way back to Temple Bar, Steph and Bianca had disappeared. Inside the Internet café, she slipped two euros into the coin slot and opened up her hotmail account. There were two emails from Jackson and she felt that warm, electric tingle that thinking of him always brought.

It was so good to have one person she could tell everything to, one person who knew all her secrets.

I keep thinking I'll see him any moment. It's crazy. I don't even know what he looks like. Except for one old photo. And it shouldn't matter that I can't find him. I've been fine for 14 years without him. I guess I shouldn't worry about it. Sorry, this is a stupid email. Hope everything in Sydney is cool. MLK

She pushed the Send button and then browsed through the rest of her emails. As she started to log off, a new message popped into her mailbox. Jackson. It was short, to the point and exactly what she needed to hear.

Hey MLK. It is important. Go for it. Find him. xxxxxxx Love you all ways, JDT

30

Chameleon man

Maeve headed back to the B&B as if she were walking on air. She knew she was late but she couldn't care. She started quietly singing a Bright Eyes song, *'This is the first day of my life . . .'* People turned to stare at her, but it only made her want to sing louder. Jackson had said she should find her father. Jackson had said he loved her.

Steph was in their room, trying on different items of clothing and flinging the rejected pieces onto the bed. Maeve longed to tell her about Jackson but it was so tied up with the search for her father that she couldn't think how to explain one without the other. Before she could say anything, Steph spoke.

'You are going to be in deep trouble. They've all left for the theatre tour. McCabe had to stay back to find out what happened to you.'

'Well, why are you still here?'

'Ben's coming to get me. He's in Dublin and I'm spending the afternoon with him. Just the two of us. He'll be here any minute!'

'You don't need to get so stressed out,' said Maeve. 'It's only your brother.'

'My brother who nearly died. My brother that I thought was dead,' said Steph. 'How's this look?'

She had on a pink hooded windcheater and black jeans and looked the same as usual, but Maeve could see she needed reassurance. 'You look nice, Steph.'

Downstairs in the front sitting room, Ben and McCabe were waiting for them. Steph hugged Ben and squealed when he lifted her up in a bear hug.

'Back by six sharp, please, Ben. We have a show to go to at the Abbey Theatre tonight,' said McCabe.

'No worries,' said Ben.

'And you and I, Maeve Kwong, we need to have a serious talk. It's not acceptable for you to go off on your own and you should know that. Everyone on this tour has to co-operate by being on time, every time. You've put me in a really awkward position. I had a number of personal commitments this afternoon and now I'm going to have to cancel them so I can take you chasing around Dublin, trying to catch up with the rest of the group.'

'Maeve could come with us,' said Ben. 'We're doing our own mini-tour of Dublin. It would be nice to have Maeve along as well. As long as that's okay with you?'

Maeve looked at McCabe beseechingly. She'd much rather spend the afternoon with Steph than have to drag around in pursuit of the rest of the group and get a lecture from Ms Donahue as well. McCabe ran one hand through his hair and sighed.

'Thank you, Ben,' he said, looking relieved. He turned to Maeve. 'But don't think this lets you off the hook, young lady.'

Out in the street, Ben's car stood waiting. 'Bags the front

seat!' said Steph as she skipped towards it, but then she stopped, confused, as a woman got out of the driver's seat.

'Margaret,' said Ben. 'I'd like you to meet my little sister Stephanie and her friend Maeve. All the way from Oz.'

'Oh,' said Steph. 'I mean, hi.' She grimaced as she climbed into the back seat with Maeve.

'Sorry,' whispered Maeve. 'For tagging along like this.' She could see the day wasn't turning out the way Steph had envisaged.

'Hey, it's okay,' said Steph. 'I'm glad *you're* here,' she whispered, shooting a look of annoyance at Margaret.

'I'm going to take you on the "other Dublin" tour. The places your old schoolteacher won't show you,' said Ben, turning and flashing a grin.

He drove out of the city along winding, tree-lined roads. At the top of a hill he pointed to a long wall with a tall bronze gate. 'That's Bono's house. You want to hop out and have a look?'

Steph shook her head. 'No thanks. He's okay but he's kind of last century.'

Ben and Margaret laughed. 'If Bono doesn't impress you, maybe the tower will,' said Margaret. 'You ever heard of James Joyce? The famous Irish writer.'

'No,' said Steph flatly.

'Oh well. You will one day. That's his tower, where he went to write,' said Ben, looking to Margaret for affirmation.

Steph scrunched up her face. 'Ben, you don't have to impress me with anything. I'm just happy that you're alive and coming home soon.'

Ben coughed into his hand and then turned the car

around. They parked at a beach and bought a packet of fish and chips. Sandy mudflats stretched to a shimmering line where two big boats were moored and the harbour was layered in soft greys, blues and purple. The clouds reached down like smudgy thumbprints against the afternoon sky.

Ben picked up a stone and sent it skipping across the still, silvery water. When he sat down on the low sea wall between his sister and Margaret, he winced.

'Does it hurt much? Where you got wounded?' asked Steph. 'Are you going back to Iraq soon, or do they think you should have a longer rest?'

Ben looked away. 'I haven't been able to tell Mum and Dad about it yet. I'm not going back. Ever. I'm finished with the army.'

'But Dad will go crazy. He was so proud of you. And I've had to defend you. When people say you're fighting a crap war, I've stuck up for you.'

'Look, Steph, all wars are crap.'

'But Dad—' began Steph.

'I can't live Dad's dream for him. I can't live my life worrying about his pride and what he thinks is important. I've changed, Steph. I don't want to be a soldier any more.'

'He's a good man, your brother. He's not taking the soup,' said Margaret.

'What's that supposed to mean?' asked Steph.

'It's an old Irish saying – that you sell out for the sake of the soup. The Protestant churches, during the famine, they offered soup so that the Catholics would give up the faith. So that's taking the soup. But your brother, he's a brave man. He's following his heart. You should respect him for it.'

'There are things I need to do here in Dublin, Steph.'

'But what about coming home?'

'Home's with Margaret now,' said Ben.

'With Margaret?' echoed Steph.

Ben looked at Margaret and raised an eyebrow, then he took Steph by the arm and walked off with her along the beach. Maeve and Margaret waited by the sea wall while Steph and Ben stood arguing on the shoreline.

'Families! God love 'em. Can't live with them, can't live without them,' said Margaret, trying to make light of it, though Maeve could tell she was upset. They sat in silence for a while, picking at the chips and waiting for Ben and Steph.

'Ben said you work in a gallery,' said Maeve, trying to make conversation.

'Just a small one. We represent local artists mostly. Though we've got an exhibition of work from a fabulous Japanese artist at the moment. You should come by and have a look.'

Maeve was annoyed. 'I'm not Japanese,' she said. 'I'm half-Irish.'

'I'm sorry, Maeve, I didn't mean it like that. I can't seem to say the right thing this afternoon. Steph must think I'm a right pain in the arse,' said Margaret, her voice full of misery. Suddenly, Maeve felt sorry for her.

'It's not you,' said Maeve. 'It's my fault too. Steph thought she was going to have Ben all to herself, that's all. He's her favourite brother.'

'He's pretty special,' said Margaret, smiling shyly. 'He came into the gallery one day and I thought he was lost. You don't get many soldiers wandering into our gallery, taking the art seriously. But Ben was different.'

Maeve pulled her knees up against her chest. 'I like looking at art too. Working in a gallery would be way cool.'

She looked over at Margaret and felt a sudden impulse to confide in her. 'My mum was kind of arty. She was a fabric designer.' She fished around in her bag, pulled out the silky green notebook and opened it carefully on the first few pages that showed the pictures of Weaving Girl intertwining threads of cloud to make patterns in the sky.

'This is one of her pictures, from when she was a student,' said Maeve, offering it to Margaret.

Margaret took the book and studied the design. 'It's lovely, Maeve. I like the way she's made parts of the cloud into a pattern of Irish knotwork.'

Maeve took the book back and stared hard. 'I didn't know that's what it was. She had a friend who was Irish. I wish I could meet him. You don't know anyone called Davy Lee, do you?'

Margaret laughed and Maeve wished she hadn't asked.

'Oh, probably about half a dozen,' said Margaret. 'Lee is a very common name.'

Maeve flipped to the page that held the photo of her father. Covering all the writing with her hand, she showed the photograph to Margaret. 'This is what he looked like. But it was a long time ago.'

Margaret glanced at the photo and then did a double take. She leant closer and laid her fingers over the thick mane of dreadlocks so only the face was exposed.

'Sure, but it's a small world. You wouldn't believe it, but I do know your Mr Lee. What a devil he looked back then, with all that hair! He always was a bit of a chameleon but there's no mistaking those eyes. Your Davy goes by the name Diarmait Lee these days and he lives over in the west of Ireland. I went to an exhibition of his paintings last summer. Fancy your mother knowing him! Do they keep in touch?'

Maeve had shut the green notebook and was holding it against her chest. She felt as if all the blood was draining out of her into the cold sand at her feet. It took her a moment to find her voice and even then she spoke with difficulty.

'My mum, she died in a car accident last year. Maybe he doesn't know. I wanted to tell him in case he hadn't heard,' said Maeve, hanging her head to hide her confusion. She hadn't really expected Margaret to know him.

Margaret reached into her handbag and pulled out a business card.

'I'm not meant to give out clients' numbers. But if you call me at the gallery tomorrow, I'll see what I can do.'

Bianca was the only one who was talkative on the way to the theatre that night. They walked through the dark streets back to the north side of the river where they were to attend a production of a classical Greek play. The rest of the group had toured the backstage of the Abbey Theatre and she was keen to give Maeve and Steph a blow-by-blow account of everything they had missed.

'*Iphigenia at Aulis*,' read Bianca from the theatre notes 'is a story of sacrifice.' She stopped as she scanned the outline. 'Euuww. This is so depressing. This dude, Agamemnon, he sacrifices his daughter so that gods will help him win the Trojan War. Gross. She's only thirteen.'

In the darkened theatre, Maeve watched uneasily as Iphigenia ran to greet her father. They'd been parted for a long time, and as soon as she saw him, she threw her arms around him, full of loving excitement. But her father was planning her death, welcoming her yet all the while plotting how to trick her mother into abandoning her so that no one would try to stop his evil plan.

After the show, the girls gathered in the foyer. Ms Donahue handed out some more program notes and asked the girls about the play.

'I hoped you noted the set design and the lighting, girls. They were brilliant. Any thoughts on the performances?'

'The guy who played Achilles didn't work for me,' said Steph. 'But Agamemnon was amazing. So scary. It would be really disturbing playing opposite him. He looked so deranged. That scene where Iphigenia was weeping, begging him to spare her life, it really cut me up. Imagine having a psycho for a father.'

Maeve thought of the picture of her father, those pale eyes, the craggy, sharp features. Margaret had said he was a chameleon, but did that mean he was a bit nuts? She couldn't believe Sue would have fallen for someone evil, but what if he was just plain crazy?

31

All the dead voices

Maeve woke from a dream of ghosts. She was surrounded by them – their big, pale bodies, their tiny mouths, their hot and angry breath. The ghosts needed something from her but she pushed them away and fought to escape. It was still dark when she woke. The heater next to her bed clanked loudly and she sat up, shivering in the icy morning.

Stephanie was slow and moody over breakfast, poking her fork at the poached eggs on her plate until the yolks bled over everything. Maeve wished they were out in the day, away from the close atmosphere of the B&B. Only Bianca was cheerful, humming to herself as she buttered a piece of toast with a thick layer of raspberry jam.

The girls had a couple of hours for shopping before meeting up again for a workshop at a Dublin school of acting. Maeve couldn't wait to get to a phone booth. If only her mobile would work here, she could call Margaret right away. She bit her lip, fighting down impatience. But after she'd finally slipped away from Steph and Bianca and found a public phone, she discovered she was trembling.

Margaret's voice was warm and friendly on the other end of the line. 'Now you tell him that your mother gave you this number before she passed away. I'm not meant to be handing out private phone numbers, but as your mother was a friend of his . . .'

Maeve balanced the phone against her shoulder as she took down the number. When she hung up, she was breathing hard and fast. What if it was a wrong number? What if it led to the wrong Davy Lee? What if Margaret had made a mistake? Could he really be that one in a million? She shoved the paper deep into her pocket and started walking towards the theatre school. Suddenly, she didn't want to be in Dublin any more. She ached with longing for Sydney, to be home, to not have this choice handed to her, this phone number in her pocket, this father so close at hand.

Ms Donahue was waiting at the bottom of a flight of stairs, chatting to a tall, lanky-limbed man in a dark tweed jacket. Stephanie and Bianca were already hanging around at the top of the stairs.

'Where do you keep disappearing to?' asked Steph.

'Nowhere. I was sightseeing.'

Her two friends eyed her suspiciously but there was no time to chat. The class was about to begin.

The tweedy man introduced himself as Patrick Cassidy, drama teacher, and he gathered the girls in a circle around him.

'To begin with,' he said, 'I want you to get a sense of your own self in the space. Here you are, in this space. We exist here, now. You have to know the space you're in.'

He crossed over to Maeve and took her hand. 'Your hand, connected to your arm, connected to your entire body.' He dropped her hand. 'Now, your mother may have told you it's rude to point, but not here. Not in this class. I want you to point to that chair.' He gestured towards a bentwood sitting in a corner.

Frowning, Maeve pointed at the chair. She wished he'd picked on someone else. 'And now to each and everything in the room,' he said. 'And point with both hands. With your whole body. I want you to feel this room.'

Bianca began to smile. She looked at Maeve and raised her eyebrows.

'All of you – make your place in this room. Know the space. Come on then. What are you waiting for?'

Cassidy kept firing questions at the girls so quickly that they barely had time to think of an answer before he was asking something else. Maeve's heart started to race and she could feel a prickle of sweat on the back of her neck. She hoped he wouldn't ask her a question. But then his sharp hazel eyes focused on her.

'Why were you late?' he demanded.

Maeve blinked. How could she possibly tell the truth? But he moved on to the next girl before she could even frame a response. He was forcing questions on every girl at gunfire pace, moving from one to the next. He didn't wait for answers but the questions left the girls breathless and edgy. He strode across the room and came back with a shiny black box in his hands. Inside were sheets of paper and each girl had to take one and read its contents to the group.

'This is acting that's felt, not acting that illustrates,' he said. 'I want you to feel your story or poem in your body, feel your presence in the space, in the world – feel where you are, who you are.'

Maeve wanted to call out in exasperation, 'How can anyone know that!' She looked down at the story that she had pulled from the black box. At the top it said it was an excerpt from 'The Song of Wandering Aengus' by someone called Yeats. She read through it quickly, anxious to get it right.

> *Though I am old with wandering*
> *Through hollow lands and hilly lands,*
> *I will find out where she has gone,*
> *And kiss her lips and take her hands;*
> *And walk among long dappled grass,*
> *And pluck till time and times are done*
> *The silver apples of the moon,*
> *The golden apples of the sun.*

Maeve grew restless waiting for her turn to read the poem. She'd never been good at waiting. It was why she liked dancing much better than drama. She needed to be in motion. As she read the poem, she felt the urgency inside her growing. She had to find out where her father had been in his years of wandering.

When it came time for the break, Maeve wanted to leave and find a phone booth straight away. But as quickly as the feeling swelled, it broke again and she felt as uncertain as she had when she first wrote down her father's telephone number.

'This is so cool,' said Stephanie. 'That guy is awesome.'
'Scary if you ask me,' said Bianca. 'A total fascist.'
Maeve shrugged. 'Are you okay?' whispered Bianca, as

Cassidy signalled for the girls to start up again. Maeve was glad there was no time to reply.

For the next activity they were each handed an excerpt from a play by someone called Beckett.

'This is the work of a master,' Cassidy announced. 'A master of the Irish theatre. Of the theatre of the world. I want you to listen, not just to the words, but to the silences.'

He recited a fistful of lines, holding the spaces between them as if each were a precious moment. 'Now, girls, you take it, a line each, a line with the silences and the waiting.' He strode around the circle, drawing a phrase from each girl.

'Take it, girls, again and again. "They make a noise like wings",' he intoned.

'"Like leaves",' said Steph.

'"Like sand",' said Bianca.

Cassidy snorted. 'Feel the words! I want it to sound like an onomatopoeia, not just a noise from the back of your throat,' he shouted.

Maeve looked up and said, 'Like the noise of green water against the dock, the sound of tears falling on stone.'

'You, stop – Like the noise of *what*? This is Samuel Beckett, not something you mess with. You're not to bugger it up with some bit of faddle from elsewhere. Your line was "All the dead voices", which you missed when it was your turn, I might add.'

Maeve pulled back inside herself. She wanted to apologise but she couldn't. For a moment, she'd felt as if Sydney Harbour was inside her, ebbing against her chest.

After the class, the girls collectively breathed a sigh of relief. 'That was so cool,' laughed Stephanie. 'It was wild.'

'You just like being bullied,' said Bianca.

'No, that was what acting should be about,' said Steph. 'He treated us like real adults, real actors, not just a pack of kids from a high school.'

All of a sudden, Maeve wondered if she could ever be an actress or even an adult. It felt too much like being skinned alive. 'I think I'll stick with dancing,' she said.

Cassidy came up to Maeve. Now that the class was at an end, he was smiling, unlike the fiery taskmaster of the workshop.

'That line, the one you threw in. Now who wrote that? Where did you find it?' he asked.

Maeve bit her lip and tried to think where the words had come from.

'You should credit your sources, girl.'

'I found it inside me. It wasn't a "dead voice" or anything. It was my voice.'

32

The loudest silence

As they walked back to the B&B, Maeve spotted a phone booth with an Eircom sign on the shiny glass.

'Hey guys, I'll catch up with you,' she said. Before Steph or Bianca could react, she'd disappeared into the crowds.

She stepped into the blue-and-white booth. She wanted to phone so badly. She fingered the folded piece of paper in her pocket. At any moment she could call and hear a voice and that voice might be the voice of her father. Her lost father. Her very own father. Not someone else's father who said they loved her, but someone who was her own flesh and blood. The slip of paper grew warm as she held it inside her closed fist. All she had to do was unfold it and dial – but it was too hard, too big, too difficult. Defeated, she pushed the door of the phone booth open.

She sat in a park called St Stephen's Green, watching the old-fashioned fountain. The past seemed everywhere in this country, as if history hung in the damp air like an invisible shroud. She'd always thought that hungry ghosts were a stupid superstition – that those who were forgotten could haunt you seemed unbelievable. But just as the ghosts of her ancestors had been everywhere in Hong Kong, Ireland echoed with voices. All the dead voices kept telling her to get up off that seat, to leave the park, to go and telephone her father, but she couldn't. What if he was horrible or crazy? What if he hung up on her? She shivered, even though the sunlight was warm against her skin. White tulips were in bloom all around the park, green and white. A bed of purple hyacinth, half unfurled and glorious, spread out before her. She sat, listening to her own small, breathless sobs.

On the bench opposite her, a man in a long dark coat leant forward, his head in his hands, as if wracked with tiredness. When he sat up straight, Maeve realised it was McCabe. Great. Now she'd be in trouble on top of everything else. He'd already lectured her once, this time he'd read the riot act.

But McCabe seemed to have a lot on his mind. He got up from his seat and started pacing back and forth, as if he was thrashing out a problem, oblivious to Maeve even as he walked right past her. When he strode back again, Maeve called out.

'Sir? Is everything okay?'

McCabe turned. Then, unexpectedly, he smiled.

'Maeve,' he said simply. 'What are you doing on the Green by yourself?'

'I asked you first.'

McCabe sat down beside her and laughed. It was as if seeing her, seeing someone he knew, had changed him back into himself.

'I'm waiting for someone, but I've arrived too early and the wait – the wait is interminable. Now you can answer my question. As you know you're in trouble, the answer had better be good.'

'You didn't give me a very good answer. I'm waiting too. Except I'm only waiting to make up my mind about something. Something I think I should do, but . . .'

McCabe laughed. 'Touché. We now know as little as we did when we bumped into each other.'

He started to look distracted again, pulling off his gloves and running his hands through his silver hair.

'I'm waiting for my mother, Maeve.'

'I thought she was . . . like my mum.'

'I grew up in orphanages. I was told she'd died. For years I fought to hold onto the idea that she was still out there, that she would come for me. Finally, I came to accept that she was dead and I was an orphan. And then, when we were organising this trip, I thought I'd try and find some other member of my family. I'd hoped I had an uncle or an aunt or cousins here in Ireland, someone who could tell me about my past.'

'But you found your mum?' asked Maeve.

'Yes, I found my mother. She lives here in Dublin in a house near the canal. I spoke to her on the phone last night and she's coming here today. I think we're both a bit frightened of meeting.'

'How can you be frightened of your own mother?'

'It's not her. It's the years that lie between. All those years I thought she was dead!' Maeve could hear the anger in his voice, saw the way his hands clenched and unclenched as he said it.

McCabe turned to Maeve and the anger dissipated. 'I'm sorry, Maeve. I shouldn't be burdening you with this story. I've found a lot more than I expected and I'm not sure how to . . . how to handle it. Serves me right.'

Maeve looked at McCabe, at his long, sharp-boned face. A hank of silver hair fell forward as he put his head in his hands again.

'It's great, sir,' said Maeve. 'It's what I'd want, if I was you. I mean, I know it's big and everything, but it's just the best thing. To find someone you've lost.' She clutched the sheet of paper in her pocket and felt her heart beat faster.

'She'll be here soon.' He glanced at his watch. 'I haven't seen her in sixty years. An entire lifetime. In about ten or fifteen minutes, she'll be here.'

'Do you want me to go away, sir?'

But McCabe didn't seem to hear her. He kept checking the gate at the eastern end of the Green, glancing across the tulips and hyacinths. Suddenly, he stood up.

'I'd better go,' said Maeve, but he didn't reply.

A tiny old woman in a pale blue coat was walking up the path. Maeve quietly slipped away, heading for the park gates. As she turned into Merrion Row she caught a glimpse of McCabe towering over the small woman as they stood face to face, a blaze of spring flowers surrounding them.

Someone had spat in the phone booth and slag was running down the glass. Maeve thought about searching for another booth, but she couldn't wait any longer. When she shoved the card into the slot, her hand shook so much she could hardly dial the number. She smoothed out the little scrap of paper. It had grown damp and crumpled in her pocket. When a woman's voice answered, she hung up without saying anything and then slammed her hand against the phone in frustration. She had to try. She had to at least find out if it was the right house. Laboriously, she dialled the number again.

'Hello, I'd like to talk to Mr Lee, please. Mr Diarmait Lee.'

'Hold on, he's just here.'

As soon as she heard him pick up the phone she spoke, before he had a chance to say anything, before she had even heard his voice.

'Diarmait Lee?'

She waited in the silence.

'Yes?'

Maeve couldn't speak. She only wanted to hear him talk.

'Hello, are you still there? Can I help you?'

'Umm, my name's Maeve. Maeve Lee Kwong. I'm fourteen years old. My mother was Sue. You knew her. You and my mum . . . When you were in Sydney . . . She never told you . . .'

It was the man's turn to struggle to find words. The stillness was like a ringing. It made Maeve want to hold the phone away from her. How could silence be so loud?

Finally, he said, 'I'm your dad, aren't I?'

Maeve couldn't speak. She nodded into the receiver even though she knew it was stupid.

'You still there?' he asked, his voice deep and gentle.

'Yeah,' she said softly. Could he tell she was crying? Her breath came in small gasps.

'Where are you? You're not phoning from Australia, are you? Sure, it sounds like you're next door.'

'I'm in Dublin with my school. We're on a school trip, me and my friends.' She'd dreamt of this conversation for so long, of all the things she'd tell him about herself, and now she just sounded stupid.

'Dublin,' he breathed, long and slow.

'Yeah, Dublin.'

'How's your mum then?'

'She's dead.'

'Jesus.'

'I'm sorry.'

There was another awkward silence. She could almost hear his thoughts. How strange it must feel to be Davy Lee. To have a daughter you didn't know you had telling you her mother had died. Maeve shivered.

'Look, it's a lot to take in, you know.'

'I don't want anything from you.'

'Jesus Christ, it's not that, girl. It's just it's a lot to take in. She was beautiful, your mum. She was . . .'

Maeve dropped the phone. She couldn't talk any longer. She sank down onto the floor of the phone booth, the receiver dangling beside her, and fought back the tears. She could hear the man on the other end, calling to her.

'Maeve, are you there? Maeve?'

Wiping her eyes on the sleeve of her jacket, Maeve reached out for the phone.

'I want to meet you. We can't be talking through this blasted phone. Where are you staying?'

Maeve bit her lip. 'We're leaving Dublin tomorrow. We're going to this other school in Kerry and staying with some homestay.'

'Kerry! I'll be close to you then. I live near Dingle. Who will you be staying with?'

'I don't know. I don't know if it's allowed,' said Maeve. 'I'll think about it. I'll call you back. I promise. I promise I'll call you back.'

She didn't wait for him to reply. Her head was whirling. She put the phone back in the cradle and walked out into the Dublin morning.

33

Confessions

They left Dublin in sleeting rain. A ripple of excitement ran through the group as McCabe and his mother boarded the bus.

'It's incredible, isn't it?' said Steph. 'Like a kind of fairy story or something. The lost mother and the lost kid and they find each other. It's so cool that McCabe is bringing her with us. She must be stoked.'

Maeve watched as McCabe helped his mother settle into her seat. She seemed even smaller and more fragile than Maeve had remembered her.

'But it could be scary too,' said Bianca.

'Yeah, scary,' said Steph.

'Really scary,' added Maeve. 'Bunka, Steph, there's something I need to tell you.'

Steph and Bianca gasped as Maeve revealed everything that had been going through her mind since she'd first heard about the Irish trip.

'But why didn't you tell us before?' asked Bianca.

'Yeah, we could have done something,' added Steph.

'I had to do it alone.'

'But you asked that Margaret to help you. And you didn't even tell me!' said Steph.

'I never thought she'd know him. I was just trying to make conversation. It was a total fluke.'

'But this is great!' said Bianca. 'I can't wait to meet him.'

'Hang on!' said Maeve. 'I don't even know if *I* want to meet him.'

Once they were out of Dublin and on the motorway, the bus sped through the soft green countryside. Maeve was exhausted after her revelation and slumped back down in her seat while Steph and Bianca talked excitedly about what they thought she should do next. Roadside sculptures, like monuments from another time, stood on the green verge – a man with birds in his hands twice life-size, a fish, standing stones, and twisted modern bronzes. Beyond were fields of such a lush green that even the grass threw shadows of deep blue.

Maeve tried to eavesdrop on McCabe and his mother, in front of them. Mostly they sat quietly together, watching the view. Maeve couldn't squash down her hungry curiosity. Why weren't they talking much? She felt she had so much to say to her own father and she hadn't waited nearly as long as McCabe.

They turned off the motorway and drove through ancient villages. Everything looked so old, as if it had always been there. They stopped for lunch in a small town full of houses painted in gaudy pink, blue and purple. Ms Donahue and McCabe each took a group of girls to separate cafés. The Musketeers followed McCabe's group into a tiny, steamy tea-house, just as the clouds broke and poured icy rain on the streets.

'Great,' said Maeve. 'We'll have to wait for a table.'

But just as she spoke, McCabe waved them over. He was sitting in a window seat framed with pink, lacy curtains with a pot of tea and a plate of barmbrack between him and his mother.

'Don't be shy of joining us,' said McCabe. He stood up and organised two extra chairs. 'We're nothing to be frightened of.'

'Call me Deirdre, please, girls,' the old lady said. 'It's lovely that you and your Ms Donahue have allowed me to tag along. It must seem very strange to you.'

Bianca leant forward and Maeve could see she was about to blab, to tell Deirdre that Maeve had found her long-lost father as well. Maeve kicked her hard under the table. The silence stretched out.

Deirdre picked up her teacup and put it down nervously so that it rattled on the thin china plate. 'I know what you're probably thinking, girls. I know you're thinking how could a mother give up her only son. But I never meant to give him up. I lost him when I wasn't much older than you. I went back to get my little boy and they told me he had died, so I wasn't to know. I wasn't to know.'

'It's all right, Mum,' said McCabe, reaching out to grasp his mother's hands.

Maeve, Bianca and Stephanie looked at each other and blushed. Bianca and Steph picked at the pale crusts of their sandwiches.

'We think it's great you're here,' said Maeve. 'Everyone thinks it's great that you and Sir found each other.'

For the first time, Deirdre smiled. 'Sir, is it? Is that what they call you, Colm? Sir?'

McCabe nodded and then suddenly they both laughed.

The bus arrived at a secondary school outside Tralee in the late afternoon. After all the old buildings, the girls had expected something at least as gothic as St Philomena's, but St Brigid's was made up of a collection of portable classrooms standing in a grassy field. The room they were taken to was obviously a science classroom but one of the long tables was laden with cakes and cups of tea.

'Don't they get sick of drinking tea all the time?' whispered Bianca. 'I could kill for a cup of coffee. They're just like the English – tea, tea, tea.'

'Or the Chinese,' said Maeve. 'My grandparents drink tea all day too.'

Ms Donahue came up to the Musketeers and drew them around her. 'Listen, girls, I think it would be really nice if we could do something to honour the occasion. The school has gone to a lot of trouble to welcome us. So I want you three to do a little performance for them. You all know "I Still Call Australia Home", don't you?'

Bianca groaned. 'You want us to sing it for them?'

'Yes, exactly. You especially, Bianca. You have a beautiful voice. Remember, this is a performing arts tour!'

The girls looked at each other and then dutifully followed Ms Donahue to the front of the science room. Bianca stood in the middle and Steph and Maeve flanked her as they bellowed out the song. Maeve shut her eyes as they repeated the chorus. Would she still call Australia home if she met her father? What if he asked her to live with him? What if she had to start calling Ireland home?

When they'd finished the song, the audience burst into applause, shouting and hooting their appreciation. Then a tall, skinny boy came to the front of the class. His face was a mass of freckles and he kept his head down so his curly brown hair fell across his eyes. One of the teachers introduced him as Fergal O'Sullivan.

'We're going to respond to your lovely performance with a bit of traditional Irish dancing. Young Fergal is going to perform a broom dance.'

The boy looked up and grinned shyly at his audience before starting a complicated manoeuvre with a broom. Maeve thought it was the weirdest dance she'd ever seen. He leapt over the broom and twirled it to one side, narrowly avoiding the Bunsen burners on the lab bench. When he'd finished, everyone applauded and some of the students yelled out his name, until he blushed again.

Maeve was glad when they were led out of the school by their homestay host, a pale, red-headed girl called Hannah.

'C'mon then. Mam will be waiting at the gate,' said Hannah. She picked up one of their bags and they all dashed out through the rain to where a battered little blue car stood by the kerb. After a hurried introduction, they squashed into the back seat alongside Hannah's little brothers and sister. Maeve was sure she wouldn't be able to remember any of their names.

'Wow, this place is so cute,' said Steph as they crossed the threshold of Hannah's house. The front door opened straight into the living room and Hannah's brothers tumbled over the doorstep and immediately began wrestling on the stone floor.

Hannah's mother stepped over their bodies. 'Don't mind the boys. Come and make yourself at home.'

She went to the wood stove that was set in an old-fashioned chimney and kindled it. Then she put a lump of peat on the sticks.

Tea was already set out on a table in the back kitchen – kippers and cheese and dark, seedy, brown soda bread. Maeve thought it was delicious, though she could see that Steph and Bianca weren't so sure.

'You make yourselves at home, girls,' said Hannah's mother.

'Maeve's family is from around here,' said Bianca.

One of the boys laughed through a mouthful of bread and cheese and the crumbs went shooting out over his lap.

Hannah's mother reached across and slapped him on the arm. 'Mind your manners, Liam,' she said. Turning back to Maeve, she asked, 'You've got a drop of the Irish in you, then?'

Maeve could see they didn't believe her, that they thought she looked one hundred per cent Chinese. It wasn't lost on Maeve that there hadn't been a single Asian student at St Brigid's. Even in Dublin, there had been plenty of Africans but not many Asians.

'Maeve's dad is Irish, isn't he, Maeve?' said Bianca.

'So that explains your name. I wondered about it. We spell it M-e-d-b, not like how you write it, but she's the same queen.'

'My dad's called Diarmait Lee. He lives near Dingle.'

'Ahhh, Diarmait Lee, you say? Now I see. Sure, if I didn't see his paintings just the other week hanging in a restaurant in Tralee. Strange they are but very lovely. And if Diarmait Lee is your father, that makes sense of it.'

Maeve nodded uncomfortably. She had no idea what his paintings looked like or where they were hung. Obviously they didn't think it strange that Diarmait Lee had an Asian-looking daughter.

'And I suppose you'll be visiting your dad, then?' asked Hannah.

Maeve squirmed in her seat. All these questions. She wanted to thump Bianca for her good-natured blabbing. 'Maybe,' she said, and then she fell silent, picking at the salty kipper on her plate.

That night, Maeve and Steph shared a double bed while Bianca slept on a rolled-out mattress on the floor beside them. Hannah and her sister had given up their room and gone to sleep in the same tiny room as their brothers.

'Listen, guys, you have to shut up about my father. I so wish you hadn't told Hannah and her family,' said Maeve. 'I don't even know if I'll be able to see him.'

'Why not? We met up with Ben, didn't we?'

'But it's different. Your parents wanted you to meet up with him. I'd have to have my grandparents' permission. McCabe will flip if I ask him to talk to Por Por.'

Steph turned onto her side and stared at Maeve in the half-light. 'Why are you making this so hard for yourself?'

'Because it's the hardest thing I've ever had to do and maybe, maybe I don't want to do it.'

She turned onto her side and shut her eyes tight, trying to imagine that she was home in Sydney. But where was 'home'? The boarding house? The flat in Potts Point? Her old bedroom back in Balmain? There was nowhere that was completely home any more. She tried to think of the things that made Sydney home. She saw herself at dance class, spinning across the old school hall while the fans spun lazily above her. She imagined sitting beneath the jacarandas at St Phil's with Steph and Bianca, or tumbling in the grass with Jackson at Coogee. She saw her grandparents at the breakfast table, Por Por fixing her a cup of tea while Goong Goong shook out the newspapers and smiled at her over the top. And she imagined lying in the folding bed beside Ned's cot, the warm, sweet, comforting smell of him. She held him in her mind's eye as if she was really holding him in her arms, and sleep came to her at last.

34

Full circle

The next morning, while they were being shown around Tralee, Maeve made sure that she fell behind so she could walk with McCabe.

'Sir?' she said. 'I need to ask you something.'

McCabe tried to smile, but Maeve could see his mind was far away.

'Are you okay, sir?'

He ran a hand through his hair. 'We had a rough night last night, my mother and I.'

'Isn't the B&B you're staying in any good?'

He hesitated before he spoke. 'Maybe you'll understand, Maeve, because you know what it means to lose a parent.

'Last night, my mother came to my room. I was already in bed, reading, and she came to say goodnight. To kiss me goodnight. All through my growing up, I used to pray, every night, that my mother would find me. When I was a little boy, I used to fantasise about having her come to my bed in the orphanage and tuck me in. And here I am, an old man, and my mother, at last, she's there with me. I wanted to laugh at the irony, but then I saw the grief of it was breaking my mother into pieces. You see, every night, since she put me in St Bart's, the orphanage I grew up in, every night, she's prayed for me. Not for the growing boy, nor the living man, but for my soul. She thought I was dead. She'd gone back to the orphanage and they'd told her I was dead!

'So here she was, fifty-eight years later, come to say goodnight to her son, and she started to weep. For all those lost years. The things she's missed! The things we both missed out on! I'd always thought I was the one who suffered – a boy without a mother – but she was broken, utterly broken by it. The waste of it all. She never had the chance to meet my wife, Gabrielle, never had the chance to see her grandsons grow up. I was all she had, and she's led her whole life alone. I'd never thought . . .'

Maeve reached out instinctively, but he pulled away and brushed his hand across his face.

'So she started weeping, grieving for all those years without me, and then she couldn't stop. I held her in my arms as if she was a little child. All night, she wept. I didn't know. I didn't understand it would be like this for her.'

Maeve felt a cold twist in her chest, as if her heart had stopped beating for a moment. What if it was like that with her father? What if he fell apart? Or what if she did?

They walked on in silence, neither of them listening to the chatter of the other girls ahead of them or Ms Donahue's directions.

'I'm sorry, Maeve. It wasn't appropriate for me to tell you all that. What were you going to ask me?'

Maeve looked up at his weary face. 'Nothing. It doesn't matter.'

The other girls chatted loudly, jostling each other as

they queued for tickets. Maeve drifted through the cultural museum in a daze, hardly paying attention to any of the displays. When they finally had some free time, she walked straight to the nearest phone booth. She fingered the phone card for a moment before pushing it into the slot.

Foxy John's was in the main street of the town of Dingle, a dusty, battered-looking pub that also doubled as a shoe repair shop. Maeve saw McCabe raise his eyebrows questioningly at her dad's choice of venue. She knew he was taking a risk in bringing her to Dingle. It was definitely bending the rules to exempt her from the planned program, especially without her grandparents' permission.

Steph and Bianca were beside themselves when they found out that Maeve had arranged to meet up with her father and that she'd talked McCabe into taking her there. They couldn't believe that they were going to have to spend a day in school joining in on classes and watching another broom-dancing demonstration while Maeve and McCabe went to meet Maeve's father.

McCabe and Deirdre took a table at the back of Foxy John's beside a workbench piled high with leather scraps and old boots. They each ordered a shandy while Maeve sat on a stool near the door of the shop, watching the street.

A short, wiry, bald man stared in through the window at her. Was that him? Was that her dad? She felt like the little bird from the Beginner Books chirping 'Are you my mother?' at everyone, pathetically searching for a parent that she couldn't even recognise. She stared hard at every man who entered the shop but most of them were only dropping off something for repair or stopping by for a quick midday pint to slake their thirst.

Maeve pressed her hands against her face, and then rubbed her eyes until they stung. She didn't feel like crying. It wasn't tears that were swelling inside her but an explosion of emotion. When she looked up again, a man was standing at the window, staring in at her. His dark hair was cropped close to his scalp but his pale eyes were unmistakable. The high cheekbones, the wide crooked mouth, all the features of her own face that she used to feel were mismatched, that made her different from her mother, here they were in this stranger's face. She folded her hands in her lap and stared back, watching calmly as he walked through the narrow double doors. The bell above the door tinkled and then he was beside her. He towered over her. She hadn't imagined him being so tall. She stared up into a face so familiar and yet so strange it made her catch her breath.

'Maeve?'

She kept staring at him, mute. Should she call him Dad? Or Diarmait or Mr Lee? She nodded, suddenly terrified that he was going to embarrass her in front of the entire café by hugging her. But he didn't touch her. He simply sat down on the bar stool beside her. Every now and then they glanced across at each other and smiled shyly. Then he reached along the bar and folded his big, strong hands over hers.

'Thanks,' he said.

'For what?'

'For waiting. I've been walking up and down the street for these past ten minutes, trying to get the courage to come and face you. Thank you for having the courage to find me.'

'It wasn't so brave.'

He smiled at her and the silence between them stretched out like a great abyss that she knew one of them would have to leap across.

'We've been studying this play,' she said. 'We had to read out bits of it in this drama workshop in Dublin. It's called *Waiting for Godot*, but you know, he never comes. I didn't want to wait for ever to find you. I'm not very good at waiting.'

'Like your mother. She was always one for chasing fate with a stick.'

Maeve frowned, not sure if that was a good thing. As if he read her thoughts he said, 'It was her great strength, the way she took hold of what she wanted. Not like me. I was a drifter. When things got too hard, I'd move on. I never stayed long enough in one place to catch hold of a dream. It all slipped through my fingers.'

Maeve had thought she'd want to ask him everything – why he left, if he'd guessed that Sue was pregnant, if he would have stayed if he'd known – but all she could do was gaze at him, as if he might vanish if she looked away.

He ordered two pints of Guinness, and when they arrived he set one down in front of Maeve.

'I'm only fourteen,' she said, staring at the thick, dark brew with the creamy, foaming head.

'Are you not allowed to be drinking Guinness? I'm sorry, darlin'. I should have made to meet you somewhere grander than this. I don't know why I said Foxy John's. There's some swanky cafés down by the harbour and here

I've dragged you into my old haunt instead.'

Maeve took a sip of the bitter, dark Guinness. 'No, I like it. I mean the place, not the beer. Maybe you finish the Guinness and I'll order a Coke.'

She was a little startled when he emptied both pints before she'd even started her drink.

'Let's get out of here, into the air where we can talk.'

'I'd like it, but could I bring my teacher?'

He looked puzzled. 'He drove me from Tralee,' she reminded him. 'I told you he would.'

She led her father to the table at the back of the pub.

'Diarmait Lee, this is my music teacher, Mr Colm McCabe, and his mum Deirdre,' she said.

'No, call me Davy. I sign my work Diarmait but my friends call me Davy.'

'Mr McCabe is Australian but Deirdre's from Dublin. They're a bit like us. They've only just found each other, too,' said Maeve.

'Sure, if everyone doesn't come back to Ireland to find their roots,' said Davy.

As they left Foxy John's, a wind swept down the street, rich with the smell of the sea, brisk and clean.

'Do you fancy a walk and I'll show you a bit of the town?' said Davy.

Maeve was glad to have an excuse to be moving. It was good to be outside, to be stretching her legs and buying time to think.

McCabe and Davy started talking about the town, its history and its future while Maeve walked behind with Deirdre. She was glad that she didn't have to do all the talking, that she could simply spend time watching her father, the way he moved, the way he laughed, the way he talked with such animation when McCabe asked him a question.

'Can you manage a walk, Deirdre?' asked Maeve.

'It's a fine thing to be walking in the open air. Colm and I can walk the streets of Dingle, the streets of Dublin, we can walk together anywhere in the world and no shame to it. No one to tell us otherwise, is there?' The old woman laughed, as if she'd just told the funniest joke. She looked different to when she'd first walked onto St Stephen's Green – taller and even younger, as if a weight had been sloughed away.

Davy led them up a twisting track behind the town that quickly grew narrow and tussocky. He and McCabe stopped and sat on a stone wall, waiting for the others to catch up.

'Why did we come up here?' asked Maeve, helping Deirdre to sit beside them.

'Colm said he was interested in the history. This is a favourite place of mine. I come up here sometimes to think about the luck of the Irish. Behind us, this field, this is a famine cemetery.'

Everyone turned to gaze at the small paddock. It looked like nothing more than lumpy ground surrounded by a low stone wall.

'Why aren't there any crosses? Why isn't there anything to mark the graves?' asked Maeve, bewildered.

'At the height of the hunger, they buried their dead without ceremony. They laid them in trenches. Maybe five thousand lie here. It's a sad, secret place, but Ireland's full of secrets.'

'Was I a secret? Did you know about me? Mum said she

wrote to you but she never knew if you got her letters.'

'No, darlin', you would have heard from me before now if I'd known. I spent ten years travelling after I left Australia. I only settled back in Ireland after your sister was born.'

'My sister?'

'Yes, and if it's all right with Colm and Deirdre, I'd like you all to come back to my house and meet her.'

It was such a weird idea. She had a sister, just like she had Ned. And she supposed she had a stepmother too. Which was an even weirder idea. An instant family. She'd thought she'd be the only one, his only daughter.

'Do you feel up to it?' he asked, almost shyly.

35

Third burren

As they walked down from the famine cemetery, Davy
dusted off his hands.

'Maria will be wondering what's become of us.'

'Maria?' said Maeve.

'That's the wife.'

He pulled out his mobile phone and made a quick call.
Then he turned to the three of them.

'Will you follow me?' he said to McCabe. 'You have to
turn down a right muddy *bothereen*, but it's only a short
drive.'

Maeve rode up front with her father in a rattling green
Renault while McCabe and his mother followed behind in
the slick hire car. There was a pile of canvases in the back
seat of the Renault and a box full of rags that were sharp
with the tang of turpentine and paint. Maeve tried to make
out what the images on the canvases were, but could only
see swirling dark colours and the limb of a man merging
with a wing.

She was glad to get out and open the old gate, leaping
over muddy puddles and then waiting for the two cars to
pass. She expected the farmhouse to be a whitewashed

cottage tucked in the folds of green hills like Hannah's house, and was surprised to find that only a corner of it was a cottage. The rest was a bright, clean modern extension built of glass and stone.

They kicked off their muddy shoes at the door and Davy called out 'Hello' as he crossed over the threshold. A small girl with white-blonde hair pounced on him, shouting 'Daddy! Daddy!'

Maeve stared at her, trying to see how they might resemble each other. But the girl was like an Irish pixie with thick, curling hair and bright blue eyes.

A tall blonde woman came out from the kitchen, wiping her hands on a cloth, and tousled the little girl's hair before kissing Davy on the cheek.

'You must be Maeve,' she said, taking Maeve's hands in her own.

'Maeve, this is my wife, Maria,' said Davy. 'And your little sister, Bella.'

'Hi,' said Maeve. 'I hope it's okay, turning up like this.'

'We're delighted, Maeve. Bella's been dying for you to get here.'

Maeve touched Bella lightly on the tip of her turned-up nose.

'We both have freckles,' she said.

'Are you my big sister, then?' asked the little girl. She stepped up close to Maeve and took hold of her hand. 'C'mon, you have to see my room. You can sleep in my room, if you like. You can sleep with me in my bed and be my friend *and* my sister.'

She dragged Maeve over to a narrow flight of stairs built into the old stone wall.

'I'll put the kettle on,' called Maria. 'I've baked a cake. Bella, you bring Maeve downstairs again as soon as you've shown her your treasures.'

Bella talked without stopping all the way up the stairs. Maeve loved the sound of her voice, the lilt of her Irish accent and her cheeky laugh. The bedroom at the top of the stairs had sloping ceilings and a small paned window. Bella started pulling dolls out from under the rumpled bedcover.

'And this is Betty, and this one's Belinda and this one is Berfa,' she said.

'Why do they all have names that start with B?'

'Because B is best, silly,' said Bella. She giggled.

Maeve knelt on the little girl's bed and peered out through the paned window. Across the fields lay Ventry harbour, a darkening blue in the late afternoon sun.

'That's where Daddy lives,' said Bella, pointing to the distant beach.

'No, your daddy lives here,' said Maeve. Though she wanted to say 'our dad', she couldn't make herself say it out loud.

'No, he doesn't. Only sometimes. Daddy, he lives there,' said the little girl, jabbing her finger against the window pane and pointing to the beach.

It took Maeve ten minutes to convince Bella to come downstairs again. She was as stubborn as Ned and much better at arguing the point. At the bottom of the stairs, Maeve stopped before a huge landscape painting of fields and sea.

'See the girl up in the sky?' said Bella, pointing at the picture. 'That's me.'

Maeve looked closely at the swirling clouds that covered the top half of the canvas. A woman's face was subtly embedded in the paint, her long hair woven into the texture of the clouds. Maeve caught her breath. The face looked nothing like Bella. The almond-shaped eyes of the cloud woman definitely belonged to Sue. Maeve smiled and led Bella into the sunny living room.

The adults chatted quietly as they sat around a scrubbed wooden table. Thick slices of fruitcake lay on a platter and everyone sipped cups of steaming hot tea. Maeve sat opposite Davy and tried not to stare. It was so hard to act normally, to strike a balance between ignoring him and swallowing him up with her eyes.

'Bella says you don't live here,' she said.

Maria looked across the table and raised her eyebrows archly. Davy laughed and swooped on Bella, wrestling her onto his knee. Maeve felt a stab of envy. It was too late for her. There were so many things that she would never share with her father.

'Well, there's truth and not in Bella's story,' said Davy. 'I've never been good at staying in one place. There are two types of Irishmen, the ones that are bound to the land, with the good earth in their souls, and then there are the rest of us, the kind you find all over the world, children of the wind. I'm the wind-blown kind, Maeve.

'When I was a young man, in the 1980s, there was a recession here in Ireland. Not like now, with Ireland in the EU and the Celtic Tiger roaring like we're all going to be rich as Midas. That's why I was in Australia and how I came to meet your mother. The street people of London, so many of them are the lost Irish of the 1980s. See, we're good at losing our way. Maria, she knows what I'm like and she puts up with me.'

'So you don't live here? You're not a proper family?' asked Maeve. As soon as the words were out she wished she'd bitten her tongue. What was a proper family anyway? But no one seemed to take offence.

'I have a truck,' said Davy, 'down at the caravan park near Ventry. I keep it parked above the dunes. I can get up in the mornings and be painting at first light.'

'I don't get it,' said Maeve. 'You have this great house and you live in a campervan?'

'Why don't you take Maeve down to Ventry and show her?' said Maria.

'We'll have to be heading back to Tralee soon,' said McCabe, glancing at his watch.

'Please, sir,' said Maeve. 'My dad and me need to be alone for a bit.'

The adults all looked at each other. Then Davy slapped his knee and stood up.

'I want to come. I want to come!' shouted Bella, throwing her arms around Davy's legs. But Maria peeled her off and held the wriggling girl firmly on her knee. 'No you don't.'

The salt and sand stung Maeve's cheeks until they tingled as she and Davy walked along the beach.

'When you come back, I'll take you out in my corrach,' said Davy. 'There's a dolphin in the bay, and sure if he doesn't love to say hello.'

'Come back?' asked Maeve.

'You can always come back, Maeve. And you will, everyone comes back to Ireland. You have roots here.'

'I don't know – there weren't many people in Dingle who looked anything like me.'

'Sure, they're not half as lovely as you, with their pasty skin and mousy hair. But that doesn't mean you can't find a place for yourself here. Your mam told me a Chinese saying once that I've always remembered. She said, "The cunning hare has three burrows."'

'Did Mum really say that?'

'Sure, that girl could recite Chinese proverbs all day.'

'Get out. She said you were the one who was always reciting poetry – Irish poetry.'

Davy laughed. 'She told you that, did she? What else did she tell you about me?'

Maeve thrust her hands deep into her pockets. 'Not a lot.'

'Good. Then we can start fresh,' said Davy. Maeve looked at him and noticed a long, narrow blue scar running from above his eye all the way to his chin. In profile you could almost mistake him for a pirate. Was there something her mother should have told her?

Davy's truck was parked on a crest of dunes among long, pale grey-green grass. It was painted dark red and a smoking, blackened stove-pipe poked out of the roof. Inside, it was not at all what Maeve expected. A double bed with a carved surround was built into one end of the truck and a beautiful carved table and chairs were set into the wall. There were sketches and small paintings scattered everywhere – strange, swirling pictures of creatures that were neither human nor beast. Some had wings, others had fins coming out of the side of their faces and still others had black knives plunged into their chests.

'We can sit on the beach, if you'd rather,' said Davy.

'No, it's like a hobbit's house,' said Maeve. 'I love it.'

Davy shut the door against the wind and stoked the small Aga stove. From a cupboard set in the wall, he pulled out a bottle of whiskey and poured himself a glass.

'I don't suppose you'll be drinking the whiskey,' said Davy. He reached back into the cupboard and pulled out a handful of small bottles of Italian sodas.

'Bella's favourites,' he said, pushing the bottles across the table toward Maeve. As he did so, Maeve saw more scars, blue lines like a strange pattern of lightning bolts running the length of his forearm.

Davy followed her gaze. 'Your mother didn't tell you about these?' he said, stroking the scars. Maeve shook her head.

'It happened in Sydney. Sue had arranged for me to meet her parents. I wasn't ready. I knew they didn't like the idea of me. She threw one of those proverbs at me. "If you do not brave the tiger's lair, how can you capture the cub?" Sure, if that wasn't guaranteed to drive me crazy.' Davy looked out the window at the sea, remembering.

'You met Goong Goong and Por Por? My grand-parents?'

Davy poured another shot of whiskey into his glass. 'I met them. But before I did, I got completely smashed, utterly legless. I was thinking how they probably wished I wasn't a white man and that their beautiful daughter should be loving a Chinaman and not a no-good Irishman. So I painted myself blue all over. Sure it was a great joke but then I walked through a set of plate-glass doors at the entrance of the bleedin' Chinese restaurant. Right at the last, just before the glass shattered, I covered my face with my arms. You can see the way the shards sliced up my arms.

When Sue and your grandfather took me to Emergency, the blue paint was stitched into the cuts. Instant tattoos.'

'My grandfather took you to the hospital?' asked Maeve. She couldn't make a picture of it in her mind. Davy covered in blood and blue paint, bleeding all over the back of Goong Goong's BMW. No wonder Goong Goong thought he wasn't 'suitable'. She laughed out loud. Davy looked relieved.

'There you have it,' he said, slapping the table. 'One of my dirty secrets. I was an idiot. I'm sorry that I met your mother when I was wandering through the realm of stupid mistakes. Things might have worked out differently if we'd met when we were older.'

'Then I wouldn't be here.'

'And that would be a great loss to the world,' he said. 'Now then, I don't really expect you to be telling me all your teenage secrets, darlin' girl, but I'd like to know more about you. In fact, I'd like to know everything you're willing to tell me about the secret life of Maeve Lee Kwong.'

Maeve propped her chin on her hands and thought. And then she began, at the beginning, telling her dad everything about the fourteen years he'd missed out on.

36

A time to dance

As the hire car drove up the winding road over the Connor Pass and headed back towards Tralee, Maeve glanced out the rear window. Below them the lights of Dingle harbour had begun to twinkle, and beyond, in the deepening evening, lay the Ring of Kerry, the water sparkling as the moon rose over the landscape.

'It's a beautiful part of the world, isn't it?' said McCabe. He glanced across at Deirdre, who was sleeping in the passenger seat beside him. 'Deirdre and I hope to find a home here. I can't take her back to Australia. It's too far and it's too late to uproot her. But I want to take care of her. I need to get to know her, while there's still time.

'While you were off with your father, I talked to Maria about buying something on the peninsula. I couldn't live in Dublin, not in that wretched house by the canal. But perhaps I could bring Deirdre west and make a home for us both. There's music here, and my boys would love to come over and visit. It won't be for ever, but this is my chance to be with my mother and I'm going to take it.'

'I can understand that,' said Maeve. 'Meeting my dad . . . I can understand why you need to be with your mum. Thanks for giving me the chance, sir. I know it must have been tricky, me asking you to take me out here. I won't tell my granny. She'd be pretty pissed off.'

'I wouldn't have taken you without asking your grand-parents first,' said McCabe. 'I phoned them last night.'

'You're kidding! Por Por said it was okay?'

'I didn't speak to Lily. I discussed it with your grandfather and he gave permission. But he asked me not to tell you until after you'd met your father. Your family are fierce secret-keepers.'

Maeve looked out at the darkening countryside, the first flush of stars twinkling in the night sky. Nothing could surprise her now.

That evening, all the St Philomena's students and their hosts met at the pub for their final night in the West of Ireland.

McCabe parked the hire car behind the whitewashed building and Maeve helped Deirdre across the muddy ground.

Inside the pub logs blazed in the wide open fireplace. Bianca and Steph yelled and waved for Maeve to come and join them at their table.

'Oh-mi-god! What happened? What was he like?' asked Bianca.

'Tell us everything! Was it amazing?' asked Steph. 'Did you sort of know him, like, instantly?'

Maeve took a deep breath. 'He said I could come and live at his house,' she said.

'What? Live in Ireland?' asked Steph, stricken.

'You can't do that,' said Bianca. 'Not until you've finished school. Not until we can come with you.'

Maeve was about to explain when Hannah's mother came over to the table carrying a tray laden with pints of Guinness.

'I know you're a little bit under-age, but you can't be going back to Australia without trying a pint,' she said, setting a glass down in front of each of the girls.

'*Slainte*,' she said, raising her Guinness.

Bianca giggled and picked up her glass. '*Slainte*,' she said, nudging the others.

Maeve licked the thick foam from her lips. 'My dad bought me a pint of Guinness this afternoon, but I couldn't drink it. It tastes disgusting. Though I guess if I'm half-Irish I should get used to it.'

'There's plenty of time,' said Steph, frowning at her glass. 'Anyway, you're not really going to leave Sydney, are you?'

'Don't worry. I've been thinking about it all the way back in the car. I don't want to stay with him. It's funny, before I met him I had this idea that maybe I would move in with him straight away – that maybe he could solve everything for me. But it's not about him.'

'You're not disappointed, are you?'

'No. He was great but kind of crazy.'

'That explains a lot about you,' said Steph.

'Maybe. There were some things about him that were like me. And I've got this little sister, who doesn't look anything like me but she reminds me of Ned. She was so cute.'

'Great, just what you need in your life. More rugrats,' said Bianca. 'He probably just needs you to babysit.'

'I don't think he needs me at all. He doesn't really need anyone. He's just that sort of person. But I'm not like that. I need you guys. And I need Ned and Andy. And Por Por and Goong Goong. And Jackson. I need all of you.

'My dad talked about being blown around by the wind and I know what he means. I had this weird feeling in Hong Kong, that there was a part of me that belonged there. And I get it here too, but I think, deep down, where I really belong is with you guys in Sydney.'

Bianca and Steph giggled, clinked their glasses together and started singing 'We Still Call Australia Home'. Maeve clapped a hand over each of their mouths. 'Stop it or Ms Donahue will make us sing it for the whole bloody pub!'

Over by the bar, McCabe had settled down at the piano and struck up a tune. Someone had given Deirdre a fiddle and she sat on a chair beside him, her head tilted to one side, her eyes closed as she soaked up the music. After listening for a moment, she quickly picked up the melody and started playing. Soon a guitarist joined in and people started getting to their feet to form a *céilis*. A group of St Brigid's students tried to show Ms Donahue and the St Philomena' girls how to dance a Galway reel and everyone's cheeks were flushed, their eyes bright.

'C'mon,' said Maeve, dragging her friends to their feet. 'It's time to dance. It's time to really start living.'

Author's note

Although this novel is contemporary in its setting, it connects to three earlier novels set in the 1850s, 1890s and 1950s. In creating the character of Maeve Lee Kwong, I drew on stories of girls I know from around Australia and I thought long and hard about 150 years of Australian stories, what changes and what stays the same.

The lives of Australian children have changed immeasurably over the course of the last 100 years. Children today have more consumer power and yet are much less likely to be employed than children of earlier generations. They are more likely to be well-travelled and have more privilege and yet, in many ways, less freedom. Their families are smaller but often more complex. Maeve's life reflects these complex changes.

Like the Irish, the Chinese have made an enduring contribution to Australian history and culture, despite persecution and exclusion. In fact, both diasporas have helped build immigrant nations across the world. Maeve is heir to both these rich histories, but ultimately she is a very Australian character.

Australia, like all vibrant modern societies, is constantly changing and adapting to embrace new ideas and new influences. Sometimes that makes it easy for us to ignore the 'hungry ghosts' from our past and forget the importance of listening to their voices. In writing Maeve's story and the companion novels that form the Children of the Wind quartet, I hope to have made a small contribution to our understanding of the voices and stories that connect us across time.